Pipe

Fallen Lords MC
Book 2

Winter Travers

Rosa,
Much love!

For questions or comments about this book, please contact the author at
wintertravers84@gmail.com

Table of Contents
Acknowledgements

Acknowledgements

As always, I wouldn't be able to this without my boys..

Nikki Horn.
This one is for you, although I think you've claimed all of the Fallen Lords as your own. Slider might start getting jealous.

Chapter 1

Pipe

"What are you doing here?"

Her doe eyes connected with mine, and she slightly shook her head. "I just came over to—"

"Sugarplum, who's at the door?" Son of a bitch. Did she really have to open her mouth? It wasn't any of her business who was at the door.

Nikki's gaze dropped to the floor. Directly on my bare legs. Fuck.

"Keep your mouth shut," I growled over my shoulder. You would think this bitch would know she was only good for one thing, and it didn't involve talking.

She huffed out a frustrated breath but managed to actually keep her mouth shut.

Nikki shuffled backward, defeated. I had never seen this woman act like anything other than sassy and mouthy. Two things I normally hated in a woman, but with her, whenever she opened her mouth, my dick hardened and all I wanted was to fuck her against whatever flat surface was available. "I'm sorry," she mumbled. "I hadn't thought you would be busy."

If getting my dick sucked qualified as being busy, then yeah, I was busy. "You need something, sugar?"

She looked up and shook her head. "No. I'll just be going." She spun around, but I grabbed her arm and pulled her to me.

"Nikki, what's going on? I really doubt you just came here to knock on my door and leave."

Her eyes darted down the hallway, and her teeth snagged her bottom lip. "I was just over talking to Karmen, and I thought I would just stop over and say hi. So, hi." She gave a small wave with the hand I wasn't holding.

I call fucking bullshit. Nikki and I had spent some time together after the club scene where Morski had tried to grab Karmen. And when I say time, I mean all the thoughts of fucking the hell out of her happened in real life. "It's almost midnight, sugar. I really doubt you were just coming over to say hi."

She pulled her keys out of her pocket and jiggled them in my face. "Yup, that was exactly what I was doing. Karmen and I were just chatting, but I was on my way out." She hitched her thumb over her shoulder and pulled her hand out of mine. "So I'll just be going."

"Nikki, wait," I called. "Are you sure there isn't anything you need from me?" She was running, and I didn't know why.

She shook her head, and her voice cracked as she spoke. "No, I don't need anything from you, Pipe." A small, sad smile crossed her lips, and she disappeared down the hallway.

I couldn't get that smile out of my mind.
It haunted me.
Day and night.
I fucked up.

*

Chapter 2

Nikki

"Can I get a side of hash?"

"You put it on the ticket?"

I rolled my eyes and shook my head. "If I had, I wouldn't be asking you."

"Then no, you may not have a side of hash."

"Then you can go tell the bitchy lady at table eleven in the corner she can't have hash because she's an indecisive cow who can't make her mind up." I grabbed the ticket Bos had in his hand and squiggled *hash* on the bottom of it. "There," I growled, thrusting the ticket back at him. "The hash is on there."

"Indecisive cow?" A chuckle rumbled from his lips, and he shook his head.

I leaned into the pass-through from the counter to the kitchen. "Yes, indecisive cow. It took the woman twenty minutes of me going over the menu with her to finally decide on the poached eggs and bacon. The fact she added the hash all on her own about bowled me over. Make the hash, now." I was not prepared to go back over to her table and tell her she couldn't have hash.

Bos huffed but turned his back to me with the ticket in his hand. He knew better than to go toe to toe with me when I was in a mood. I had only been here for a month, and he already knew not to mess with me.

"Bad day, sugar?"

I gritted my teeth. I hated when anyone called me *sugar*. My eyes closed, and I leaned back my head. "For the ninetieth time, Alice, please stop calling me sugar."

She stepped next to me and bumped me with her hip. "Sorry, sugar."

"It's a good thing I like you, Alice. Otherwise, I'm pretty sure I would have tit-punched you."

She scoffed and pinned her ticket up for Bos. "Please, that would have been the most action I've had in months. The old girls would have liked the attention."

"The fact you call your boobs 'old girls' worries me."

"Would you prefer peaches and cream?" She snapped her gum and put her arm around my shoulders. "The Olson Twins?"

"Oh, my God," I scoffed. "You are completely mental, you know that, right?"

"You say mental, I say I know how to have fun." She rested her head on my shoulder and sighed. "You wanna go out tonight? I thought we could hit up The Mark and watch the latest Vin Diesel movie."

"You mean the one you've watched the past month every weekend? And by the way, Fast 8 is not a new movie anymore."

"Well, by Kales Corners standards, it is."

I pulled away from her and turned around to lean against the counter. "I think I'm going to have to pass. The last three weekends of watching the same movie over and over have kind of grown unappealing."

"Well, I suppose we could take this weekend off and do something different. Although, don't make plans for next weekend because I think they are getting the one with Mark Wahlberg in it." Alice grabbed a towel off the counter and wiped down the coffee machine. "That man is almost as dreamy as Vin."

"Why don't we go to the bar tonight?"

Alice scrunched up her nose. "Really? You'd rather go to the bar instead of the movies? There are only eighty-year-old men and college drop-outs there. I'm afraid to say the bar scene you're probably used to is way better than The Bar. I mean, they couldn't even come up with a decent name. It is literally called The Bar."

She was right about the unoriginality of the name, but I needed a drink and didn't feel like buying a bottle I was only going to have three sips out of and the rest would sit there. "We go to the bar for a few drinks, and then I promise, we can head back to your place and watch whatever Vin Diesel movie you want."

Alice tilted her head to the side and stuck out her hand to me. "Deal," she mumbled, shaking my hand. "I'll pick you up at seven. We chug our drinks, and we can be back to my house by eight."

I was going to accept that. If I drank enough, I would get drowsy and be out before we got through the opening credits of whatever movie Alice picked.

"Hash. Don't forget to write on the ticket from now on." Bos slammed down the plate behind me, and I closed my eyes. Oh, how I wished for the days of Karmen and me working together. Things were so much better back then. Now I was in this podunk town trying to heal a broken heart that never should have broken, but that was the silly thing about hearts.

They felt whatever they wanted, and there wasn't any way to stop it.

*

Chapter 3

Pipe

"Wake the hell up."

I cracked open one eye and saw the dingy, dirty wall in front of me. An audible grunt rumbled from my lips, and I closed my eye. There wasn't anything I needed to wake up for right now. After my full bottle of whiskey last night and not falling asleep until well after noon, nothing was going to get me out of this bed.

"Karmen thinks she knows where Nikki is. I need someone to ride with me."

I willed my body to not jump out of bed. This wasn't the first time Nickel had come to me with those exact same words. No one knew where Nikki had gone. She was here one day and then gone the next. After she had come to my door and heard the damn whore in my room, I couldn't talk to her. She shut me out, and I couldn't figure out how to get in. Hell, I don't know why the hell I even wanted to get in.

She should have been some girl who I had slept with, and that was that, but she wasn't. The one time we had been together was burned into my soul, and I couldn't get her gone. "Not interested," I grumbled.

Nickel yanked off my blanket, and a chill greeted me. "Thank Christ, your ass wasn't naked," he chuckled. "We leave in two hours. She's right this time."

I rolled over and looked up at Nickel. "You said that the last two times we tore out of here like a bat out of hell, and she wasn't there."

"I sent Manic and Slayer ahead. They both said she's there."

I closed my eyes and shook my head. "You sure are going to a lot of trouble to find this chick."

"She's not some chick to Karmen." Nickel moved to the door and looked over his shoulder. "And don't try to deny she's only just a chick to you too. You've changed, Pipe, and we all noticed when it happened."

"I'm not into whatever Oprah shit you're about to lay on me. I'm straight. Your ol' lady's friend doesn't matter to me." I grabbed my pillow and laid it over my face. "Get out," I muffled.

"Well, I guess that's more than you've ever said about Nikki before."

Her name rolled around in my head like it always did. The only way I lost it was at the bottom of a bottle. I yanked the pillow off my head and tossed it in the direction of Nickel. "You wanna tell me what the hell is going to get you out of my room?"

"Five o'clock, be ready." Nickel waltzed out of my room, leaving the door wide open.

Fucking hell.

I didn't want to do this shit anymore.

I had followed every lead I could to find Nikki, and none of them panned out.

My gaze landed on the clock across the room. It was three-thirty, and I had barely slept three hours. There was no way in hell I was going to be able to sleep now I knew we were going to possibly see Nikki tonight.

"Did he tell you?" Karmen peeked her head in my room. She had a huge smile on her face, and she looked like she could break out into song at any moment. "We found her."

"You think she wants to be found?" I didn't want to be a dick, but you had to wonder, if Nikki went to such lengths to disappear, if she actually wanted to see any of us again.

Karmen cocked her head to the side. "She calls me. If she truly wanted to never talk to me again, then she wouldn't call me.

She had a point. "You're relentless, doll."

"You're coming with, right?"

I sat up, leaning back on my elbows. "You really need me there?" I don't know why, but Karmen always insisted whenever Nickel got a lead on where Nikki was I needed to go along.

She had been gone a little over a month, and we had been on five wild goose chases looking for her.

She looked over her shoulder and stepped into my room. She pushed the door shut behind her and leaned against it. "Something happened, Pipe."

"With what?"

"With you and Nikki. I'm not stupid. After the whole thing at the club where Morski tried to kidnap me, things changed with you and Nikki."

"She tell you that?"

Karmen shook her head. "No. She swore up and down she wasn't interested in you."

I laid back down and held up my hands. "Then I guess you have your answer. She wasn't interested in me, so nothing happened."

She crossed her arms over her chest and paced the length of my room in front of my bed. "You think Nickel will like you being in my room with the door shut?" Not that Nickel would actually think that I would try anything with Karmen.

She tossed her hands up in the air and sighed. "You're not going to distract me from this, Pipe. Something happened to you and Nikki. Something that made her run."

"Nickel told me you said Nikki had been thinking about moving for a while."

"Yeah, but if she were going to move because she was fed up with Weston, then she wouldn't have left in the middle of the night like some thief. She left with no trace because of something that happened with you two."

"You're barking up the wrong tree, doll." I wasn't going to admit to anything. Nikki and I had knocked boots, but that was it. Neither of us had made any promises, so I wasn't going to take any blame in her running. Did I feel like an ass for having another chick in my room when she showed up? Hell yes, but I hadn't been doing anything wrong.

"No, I'm not, but I don't think you're up to admitting that just yet." She moved to the door and pulled it open. "I'm assuming Nickel told you we are leaving in an hour, right?"

"He mentioned it."

She nodded her head and slipped out the open door.

I didn't want to go.

The odd sensation she had left inside me when she disappeared wasn't getting better, but I was getting used to it. The dull, nagging ache I felt was becoming a part of me. My hand grazed my chest, trying anything to brush away the feeling.

I did that often.

Fuck it.

I was going to go. Maybe seeing Nikki again would give me closure or some shit like that. I wasn't a damn shrink, and there was no way in hell you would ever catch me talking about my feelings with some stranger, but just maybe seeing Nikki would make everything go back to the way it was.

Back to when the only person I cared about was myself.

Back to getting my dick wet with anyone I wanted.

Back to before Nikki.

*

Chapter 4

Nikki

What in the hell was she wearing?

"Um, Alice? Is that what you are wearing?" My gaze traveled over her clothes as she backed out of my duplex, and I couldn't believe what I was seeing. She had to be going back to her house to change. I had never met someone who would step foot out of the house wearing what she was.

"What? Why?" She shifted the car into drive and launched us forward toward The Bar.

It was a quarter after seven, and Alice was late, but I was used to that. Alice was late no matter what she was doing. Bos, who made the work schedule, had two schedules. One for Alice, and one for the rest of us. Her schedule was always fifteen minutes ahead of the schedule we had.

I shifted in my seat and rested my hand on her arm. "Sweetie, you are wearing a one-piece pajama suit thing in a very loud cow print."

She rolled her eyes and turned onto the main drag of Kales Corners. "I know. I'm the one who dressed myself."

"Is the dress code at The Bar nap time chic?" Although what Alice was wearing was anything but chic. "Where do you even find something like that?"

Alice snickered. "Oh, you got jokes now, huh?"

I tried wiping the smile off my face, but it was damn near impossible. "Seriously, what is with the moo moo onesie?"

"You promised we would only have a couple of drinks and then we are heading back to my place. I figured there wasn't a reason to get all gussied up only to take it off half an hour later."

I sighed and stared out the windshield. "I can see your logic, but I would have gone with pajamas that were a little bit less...well...*cow.*"

"Besides, I'm not looking to impress anyone at The Bar. Half of those guys are friends with my dad and grandpa."

Second thoughts about going to the bar flashed through my head as she pulled into the vacant parking lot. "Are you sure this place is even open?" I asked. I figured there would have been at least a couple of cars in the parking lot.

"The bar is always open. It's the only place you can get a drink around here besides the grocery store." Alice pulled up next to the door and shut the car off. "I'm telling you, you have no idea what we are about to walk into."

I pushed open my door and put one foot on the pavement. "As long as they have whiskey and a jukebox, I'll be good."

Alice rolled her eyes. "Sugar, you could have had both of those at the restaurant. You know Bos has a bottle behind the grill, and I could have brought in my boom box."

"Are we in the eighties now?" I laughed as I slid from the car and slammed the door shut behind me.

She rounded the front of the car and leaned against the fender. "Don't be talking shit about my boom box. I'm gonna bring it to work tomorrow, and we are going to liven up the breakfast crowd."

"We seriously need to update you, sweetie," I muttered. Alice was only four years older than I was, but I swear, sometimes it felt like she was twenty years older. "Now, let's get our drink on so we can safely get you back home to your movies and cow pajamas."

Alice moved to the front door and held it open for me. "After you, sugar. I want to see your expression when you walk in."

I rolled my eyes and stepped into the smoky bar. My eyes adjusted to the foggy haze. I waved my hand in front of my face and looked back at Alice who was still standing outside. "I thought you couldn't smoke inside bars anymore."

Alice laughed and hesitantly stepped next to me. "Technically, you're not supposed to, but the only people who come in here smoke, so it really doesn't matter."

My gaze traveled over the small bar, noticing the bartender leaning against the bar, a cigarette hanging from the corner of his mouth while he pointed a remote at the TV over the bar. "Three dollar rails, two dollar drafts, and one dollar pull-offs," he mumbled without looking at us.

"Gee, Reierson, it's nice to see you too." Alice strolled up to the bar and set her wallet on it.

Reierson, the bartender, looked over his shoulder and smiled. "You're the last person I would have thought would walk through that door tonight, Alice." He turned fully around to us, and his eyes bugged out of his head. "What in the hell are you wearing?"

A giggle escaped my lips knowing I wasn't the only one who thought Alice's attire was a bit mind-boggling.

Alice rolled her eyes and scoffed. "I'll have a Coke, and Nikki will have whatever will get her drunk in half an hour. The meter is running on my patience, and I have no plans to be here longer than thirty minutes."

I lamely waved at Reierson and cleared my throat. "Um, I'll just have an amaretto sour. Make it a double."

He hitched his thumb at me and smiled at Alice. "Is she always this cute?" His gaze landed on me, and he shook his head. "How about a whiskey and Coke? That's about as close as you're going to get to an amaretto sour here."

I had initially wanted whiskey, but I was trying to ease into a drunken stupor for the night. Reierson had plans for me to fall head-first into it. "That'll do," I mumbled. One does not turn down whiskey.

"Pretty dead tonight." Alice plopped down on her bar stool and slowly spun around taking in the bar. "I thought for sure at least Mick, Bean, and Dell would be here."

"They were," Reierson replied. He poured a healthy stream of whiskey into my cup and topped it off with a short squirt of Coke. "Your mama called and said she had leftover pot roast and they were out the door faster than I could add their drinks to their tabs."

Lord have mercy, I was going to be half in the bag after three sips.

Alice snickered watching Reierson's heavy hand with my drink. "You think you could maybe go light on the first drink with her?"

He shook his head and placed our drinks in front of us. "You get what I serve you. Rule number uno of The Bar."

I hesitantly took a sip and felt the whiskey burn the whole way down my throat. "Good golly," I gasped.

Alice sipped her Coke and slowly spun around in her chair. "I have a feeling we'll be out of here in fifteen minutes, and I'm pretty sure Reierson is going to have to carry you out."

That was probably a good guess. I lifted my glass up to hers and tapped them together. "Cheers, babe. Here's to forgetting, well…everything."

"There is one good thing about you deciding to get rip-roaring drunk today. I can get your lips loose, and you can tell me all about everything you are trying to forget."

I took a huge gulp and shook my head. "You could feed me that whole bottle of whiskey, and there is no way I would tell you. It's in the past, and that is where I fully intend it to stay."

Alice watched me warily as I downed half of my glass and slammed it down on the bar.

"It's a man, isn't it?" This was from Reierson.

I leveled my glare on him. "Really? Aren't you just here to get me drunk?"

He leaned his hip against the bar and crossed his arms over his chest. "I'm here for whatever you need me for."

"Ew," Alice squeaked. "You think you could turn down the creep-o factor?" She wrinkled her nose and stopped spinning.

"The offer stands for you, Alice." Reierson winked at Alice and moved down to the other side of the bar. He grabbed a towel off the bar and started drying off glasses.

I spun my chair toward Alice and grabbed her legs, stopping her from spinning away from me. "You wanna tell me what that was all about?" I asked.

She shrugged. "Probably the same thing going on with you, but since you don't want to talk about it, then neither do I."

"You're evil, Alice," I mumbled.

"As soon as you tell me what is going on with you is when I'll tell you what the deal is with Reierson. Although I'm sure, your story is going to be much more entertaining than mine."

I looked over my shoulder at Reierson who kept glancing at Alice. "I highly doubt that. I can tell that man has the hots for you."

"What you call the hots is more known as the fact we live in a small town, and he doesn't have a lot of prospects to hook up with."

I scoffed and took a sip of my drink. "I highly doubt that. I think it more has to do with the fact you are smokin' hot and he can't control himself."

Alice put a hand on my shoulder and laughed. "Sugar, he actually said out loud, 'I don't really have much of a choice' when he was asked about me."

Hell. That had to hurt. I turned my back to Reierson, not liking the way he had talked about my new-found friend. "Well, fuck him. You are way better than someone to settle for."

Alice clinked her glass against mine. "Amen, sista." She set down her glass and smiled. "And now it's your turn because I somehow told you what was going on with him without even knowing I did it."

"There isn't mu—"

"Oh, my God, I found you!"

My jaw dropped, and the blood rushed from my face. My eyes landed on the door, and if I hadn't been sitting down, I would have ended up flat on the floor.

Karmen was standing in the doorway. Nickel was next to her.

Pipe was sneering at me behind her.

Holy. Fuck.

*

Pipe

We found her.

After we made it to her duplex and found it empty, we decided to hit the local bar before we headed back to Weston. I never would have thought Nikki would be sitting on a barstool with a drink in front of her gabbing with some chick.

"She doesn't exactly look happy to see us," Nickel murmured under his breath.

Karmen took off across the bar not caring that Nikki looked like she was about to puke.

Nickel looked over his shoulder and smirked. "You still want that drink?"

No, I sure as hell didn't. Karmen had thrown herself at Nikki, but Nikki was looking at me like I had run over her puppy and was grilling it over an open flame.

Jesus, maybe her leaving did have something to do with me.

Nickel and I made our way over to the bar next to Nikki, and I nodded to the bartender.

Karmen was in the middle of running her hands over Nikki and asking her fifty questions. Karmen had said she talked to her on the phone, but she was acting like she hadn't spoken to Nikki in years.

"Whiskey, on the rocks."

Nickel held up two fingers. "Make that two."

Hell, the bartender might as well just put the bottle in front of us.

Nickel wound his arm around Karmen's waist and pulled her to his side. "Breath, baby. You're smothering her."

Karmen huffed and looked up at Nickel. "I have a month of not seeing her to make up for."

"Well, I don't think you need to do that in the first thirty seconds you see her," he chided.

She slapped him on the chest, and I swear to God, a growl escaped from her lips. "I'm gonna smother you in your sleep if you're not careful."

His hand traveled to her small bump, and his other hand caressed her cheek. "I'll come back and haunt you and this baby, baby girl."

"I see Nickel's possessive assholeness hasn't changed since I left," Nikki giggled. She grabbed her glass, downed it in three swallows and set it on the bar. "Well, this was a great reunion, but Alice and I have some plans with Vin and the guys."

The chick she was with clapped her hands like a happy seal and hopped off her barstool.

"Wait, what? You can't leave." Karmen grabbed her arm and smashed her nose to nose with Nikki. "And who the hell is Vin? You've been holding out on me," Karmen whispered.

Under normal circumstances, whenever I was in a bar, you could barely hear the person next to you talking, but Nikki had found a hole in the wall no one else knew about except for the bartender and the chick dressed like a cow.

Nikki warily sat back down but clutched her purse in her other hand. "Vin is no one, and Alice and I only planned on being here for a couple drinks."

"Nikki," Karmen pouted, "I haven't seen you in a month. You can't hang out with me for a little bit? I know you wanted to get out of

Weston, but I didn't think you wanted to get away from me." And this is where Karmen burst into tears and buried her face in Nickel's chest.

The bartender set our drinks in front of Nickel and me. I downed my drink and motioned to him to keep them coming. I bumped Nickel and handed him his drink. He kept his arm wrapped around Karmen and lifted the glass to his lips with the other hand.

"Why is she crying?" Nikki asked, bewildered. Her eyes were bugged out, and she looked back and forth between Nickel and me.

"She's pregnant," Nickel informed her as if that explained everything.

"Girl, your hormones are raging, huh?" Cow pajama girl asked.

"You have no idea," Karmen wailed.

Good lord. Karmen was having a nervous breakdown. Nikki looked like she was ready to bolt any second, and Cowgirl had a huge smile plastered on her face watching the craziness unfold.

"I'm Alice, in case you didn't catch that. Nikki and I work together." Alice gave a big wave and tipped her glass to Nickel and me. "You guys are more than welcome to come back to my house and hang out with Vin and us."

Nikki spun around and glared at Alice. "Would you stop?" she hissed. "They are not coming with us."

Karmen wiped her nose on Nickel's chest and raised her head. "Why can't we come hang out with you? I'd love to meet your boyfriend."

"Boyfriend?" Alice asked, bewildered. "You got a boyfriend and didn't tell me?" she asked Nikki.

Now the circle of confusion was complete.

"No, I don't have a boyfriend, Alice. You damn well know that. She thinks Vin is an actual guy."

"He *is* real, Nikki," Alice insisted.

"Of course he is, but he's real in California or wherever the hell it is he lives. I'm pretty sure Vin Diesel isn't sitting on your couch waiting for us, now is he?"

Nickel looked over at me. "Did we drive into the twilight zone and not know it?"

I shrugged and grabbed a shot off the bar. "I didn't notice anything on my bike. Maybe in that cage, you would have noticed."

"I wonder where he does live?" Alice pondered.

"I'll Google." Karmen pulled her phone out of her pocket.

"Wasn't she just crying ten seconds ago?" I asked.

Nickel shrugged. "Just go with it, brother."

That sounded like good advice. I wasn't up to deciphering Karmen's mood swings.

"So are we going back to my house or not?" Alice bounced on the balls of her feet with a huge smile on her face. "I already got the movie loaded. I just need to stop by the store to get more snacks since I only planned on Nikki coming over tonight."

"Get beer," Nickel advised.

"Google says New York and Los Angeles," Karmen muttered.

Alice tossed a ten-dollar bill on the bar and hitched her purse over her shoulder. "I suppose he has a couple places he lives. Nikki and I can run to the store, and we can meet y'all at my house."

"Nikki can ride with me." I don't know why I opened my mouth.

Everyone turned to look at me, their jaws dropped.

Was it so odd Nikki rode on the back of my bike with me? Nickel had offered me to ride in the cage with him, but I wasn't up for the Karmen and Nickel show.

"What do you mean by ride with you?" Alice asked.

Nikki scoffed and shook her head. "They're part of the Fallen Lords, Alice."

Alice's eyes lit up. "Motorcycles?" she asked with awe in her voice.

"Yup. I'm sure if you play your cards right, Pipe will take you for a ride." Nikki stood and hitched her thumb over her shoulder toward the door. "You guys don't really want to come to Alice's, do you?"

Karmen looked up at Nickel and clasped her hands to her chest. "Please," she begged. "We can hang out there, get a room at a hotel for the night, have breakfast with Nikki, and then we can head back to Weston in the morning."

"You got this all planned out, don't you, baby girl?" he reached up, tucked her hair behind her ear, and looked over at me. "You gonna stay or head back tonight?"

Nikki's eyes connected with mine, and I knew exactly what she wanted me to do.

I grabbed a cigarette out of my pocket and stuck it in the corner of my mouth. "I'll stay."

Nikki gritted her teeth and grimaced. "Perfect," she growled.

She grabbed Alice by the arm, and they marched out of the bar with the door slamming shut behind them.

"You gonna tell us what that was all about?" Nickel asked.

I shook my head and tossed a twenty on the bar. "Nope. But I do think we should get out there before Nikki convinces her cow print clad friend to leave without us."

Karmen grabbed Nickel's hand and tugged him toward the door. "He's right. We just found her, we can't let her get away again."

Nickel laughed and pulled his keys out of his pocket. "I don't think Pipe would let her get away again."

Karmen gave me a knowing look but wisely kept her mouth shut.

I wasn't going to let her get away again. At least, not until I figured out what the hell was going on between us. I wanted her, but I had never wanted someone like this before.

Nikki was different, and I didn't like it one bit.

*

Chapter 5

Nikki

"You have about fifteen seconds to spill."

I rolled my eyes and leaned against Alice's car. I didn't have a damn clue what the hell was going on. I had my own questions that needed to be answered.

How did they find me?

Why was Pipe with them?

And why in the hell was Pipe staying the night?

"Hello." Alice waved her hand in my face. "What is going on, Nikki? I can see you being friends with the chick, but I'm not too sure about the two guys."

"Then why did you invite them to your house?" I hissed.

"Because my mama raised me to be polite. I couldn't invite Karmen and not the two burly guys."

"Nickel is cool."

She rolled her eyes. "How great, he's cool. How about we talk about the tall drink of water who just walked out the front door and has eyes only for you?"

Shit.

Fuck.

Damn.

My plan to get in the car before Nickel, Karmen, and Pipe got out of the bar went out the window.

Pipe leaned against the back of Alice's car and cupped his hand around the cigarette in his mouth, lighting the end.

I hated how handsome the man looked while he slowly killed his lungs. I hated smoking, but whenever Pipe did it around me, it made me sigh and wish I was the cigarette in his mouth.

Argh! This man made me whacked in the head. Who in their right mind wished to be a cigarette?

He inhaled deep and turned his head to blow the smoke over his shoulder.

"Nickel and I are going to run to the hotel to get a room for the night, and then we'll be over to Alice's."

Nickel put his arm around Karmen's shoulders and tucked her to his side. "You gonna ride with us?" he asked Pipe.

He shook his head. "Nah. Just make sure there is a couch for me to sleep on."

"You wanna come to the store with us?" Alice looked at her watch. "And if you guys want beer, then we need to go now. They stop selling alcohol at eight."

Pipe took another drag and shook his head. "What the hell kind of town stops selling alcohol at eight o'clock on a Friday night?"

"The kind that lives in the stone age and has a population of five hundred," I explained. If Pipe didn't like it, he was more than welcome to go back to Weston.

"There's that sass," he mumbled.

I didn't want him talking about my sass. He used to tease me all the time about it, but that was when I actually wanted to be in the same room as him.

"Okay," Alice whispered. She moved around to the other side of the car and slipped into the driver's seat.

I rested my hand on the door handle. "Try to keep u—" My words died in my throat when I heard the Alice lock the door. I yanked on the handle, and the door didn't budge. Oh, hell no. "Alice, open this door," I demanded.

I hunched over to look in the car and saw she had a huge smile on her face and was shaking her head. "Nope. You need to catch up with your friends. I'll go to the store, and I'll meet you at your place."

"What? I thought we were going to your place."

She shook her head and started the car. "No. I'll run to the store, grab a movie from the rental place on Main, and then I'll be over."

No. I did not want them coming over to my house. That was the last place I wanted Pipe to be. "Alice, we are not going to my house."

She shook her head and shifted the car into reverse. She cranked up the radio and slowly crept the car backward.

Pipe stepped back from the car, and I tried not to think about that damn cigarette in his mouth.

Focus, Nikki.

"I can't hear you," Alice shouted. "See you in half an hour at your place!" She stomped down on the gas, rocketing the car out of her parking spot.

"I hate her," I growled as I watched her taillights fade as she pulled out of the parking lot and down the street.

Karmen clapped her hands together and gave a little jump. "Well, Nickel and I will run to the hotel, and we'll meet you at your place."

"No," I insisted. "I can ride with you guys to the hotel, and then we can all head over to my place."

"Nonsense. There's no reason why we all need to go. Nickel and I will only be a few minutes." Karmen grabbed Nickel's hand and pulled him over to her car. "You don't by chance have ice cream, do you?" she asked.

"Does it snow in Alaska?" I asked. I don't think I ever had a freezer lacking ice cream. "Cookie dough, mint chocolate chip, and butter pecan."

Karmen pumped her fist in the air. "I knew I could count on you to satisfy my weird cravings."

"Hey, hey," Nickel called as he opened her door. "The only one who is going to satisfy your cravings is me."

Karmen rolled her eyes and ducked into the car. "You're such a man," she mumbled.

"Last I checked, that was something you liked about me." He slammed her door and rounded the front of the car. "Try not to kill each other," he called.

Once again, I was watching the taillights of a car I wished I was in.

"You know, I really thought you would have been a bit more excited to see me, sugar."

I looked at Pipe and tried not think about everything that drove me crazy about him. "If I had wanted to see you, I knew where to find you."

He shook his head and inhaled deeply. The end of the cigarette burned bright, and his eyes stayed trained on me. He tossed the half-smoked cigarette on the pavement and stomped on it. "That mean you never wanted to see me again?"

Truer words had never been spoken. "It wasn't on the top of my list."

"You mind telling me why that is?"

I looked around and decided this was not the place I wanted to have this conversation. Hell, I never wanted to have this conversation with him. "No."

He shook his head and strutted over to his motorcycle. "You can't shut me down that easily. But I'll let you have a little reprieve 'til later." He tossed his leg over the bike and looked over at me. "I promise not to bite, sugar, even though I know that's something you're into."

Why that rat bastard. A smirk spread across his lips, and all I wanted to do was punch his lights out and walk home. He would, of course, bring up something from the one and only night we had spent together.

"You don't get to do that."

"Do what?"

"Act like you can talk to me like I'm someone you care about."

He frowned and tilted his head a little bit. "Who said I didn't care about you, Nikki?"

"Sometimes it's not what you say, but it's what you do."

He shook his head and cranked up the bike. He grabbed the helmet that was hanging from the handlebars and held it out to me. "Hop on."

Good. He wasn't going to argue the fact that he did care about me.

As I strapped on the helmet, I remembered the first time I had ridden on the back of Pipe's back. The feel of my legs wrapped around his strong, muscular body combined with the rumbling of the motorcycle was enough to drive me to the brink of ecstasy. When I first met Pipe, I thought he was handsome, but when my body had touched his, I went up in flames. The man was beyond hot.

"Do you know where I live?"

Pipe smirked and revved the engine. "I was just there, sugar."

I swung my leg over the back of the bike, sitting back as far as I could without falling off the back end.

Pipe looked over his shoulder. "You don't think you need to hang on?"

I gripped the seat between my thighs and shook my head. "Just don't go fast and I'll be fine." It was less than a five minute ride to my place, and there was no reason for Pipe to drive like a bat out of hell.

"Suit yourself."

Pipe rocketed out of the parking lot, and I lasted two point five seconds before I plastered myself to his back and wrapped my arms around his waist.

Damn man.

*

Pipe

I didn't want to go to her house.

The feel of her body wrapped tightly around me was something I didn't want to end. She had only been on my bike a handful of times before, but I remembered each time vividly.

Once we got to her house, I wouldn't have her to myself anymore. Karmen would squirrel her away, taking all of her time.

"What are you doing?" she hollered over the roar of the engine.

I was getting five more minutes alone with her. I wasn't familiar with Kales Corners, but it was a tiny town. It was virtually impossible for me to get lost.

By the time we made it back to her house, I knew she was pissed. Her friend was waiting on the front porch of her duplex, a perplexed look on her face and plastic bags were at her feet.

"What in the hell was that?" Nikki hissed. She catapulted herself off the bike, whipped off the helmet, and shoved it at me.

I shrugged and didn't answer. The problem was, I had no idea what that was. I wanted to be next to her, but I knew that wasn't something I should want.

"Well, gee golly. I thought for sure I was going to be the last one here." Alice scooped the bags off the porch and watched Nikki climb the steps to her. "I had no idea what kind of beer to get. So I got three different kinds."

Nikki grabbed two of the cases of beer off of the porch, pushed open the door to her house, and disappeared inside.

"You think you can grab the other one?" Alice called to me.

"Got it." I hung Nikki's helmet on the handlebars but didn't move from the bike.

Alice watched me for a few seconds, her head tilted to the side before she followed Nikki.

I hung my head and closed my eyes.

What in the hell was I doing?

*

Chapter 6

Nikki

"You have ten point three seconds to tell me what in the hell is going on." Alice dropped the bags onto the counter and stared me down.

"Nothing is going on." I grabbed a case of beer and twisted around to open the fridge.

"Oh yeah, nothing is going on. Everyone has a motorcycle club tracking them down. Totally normal," she scoffed.

"The club wasn't looking for me, Karmen was. Nickel is her ol' man." I set the beer on the bottom shelf and reached for the other case.

"You know the words *ol' man* just came out of your mouth, right? No one around here talks like that, Nikki. This is like a whole new side of you."

I shook my head, grabbed the other case of beer, set it down, and slammed the fridge shut. "I don't really think you know me that well, Alice. I've only been here one month."

Her face fell, and she fidgeted with the handle of one of the plastic bags.

Shit. I didn't mean for it to come out so harsh. "I mean, you know me, Alice, it's just there are somethings I haven't told you."

She rolled her eyes and started pulling food out of the bags. "That much is obvious."

I leaned against the counter and lowered my voice. "I honestly don't know what is going on. Well, I get why Karmen and Nickel are here. I just don't know why Pipe came with them."

Alice ripped open a bag of red licorice and held it out to me. "I knew there was something going on with you two. No way a man stares at a woman the way he did you without something more between them."

I grabbed a piece of licorice and glanced at the open door behind us. I fully expected Pipe to walk through it at any moment acting like things weren't beyond weird between us. "He wasn't staring at me."

"Of course you would think that. You didn't actually look at the man until we were outside. He couldn't take his eyes off you when he walked in the bar."

I wagged my piece of licorice at her and shook my head. "No, I don't accept that."

"What don't you accept?" Karmen asked. She had the last case of beer in her hand and kicked the front door shut behind her. "Pipe was smoking. Nickel said he'll hang out there until he's done." She dropped the beer on the counter in front of me and leaned against it. "That should give me enough time to ask you what the hell is going on between you and Pipe."

"She doesn't know either? I thought she was your best friend," Alice squawked.

"Nikki has kept her lips zipped about Pipe since whatever it was that happened, happened." Karmen crossed her arms over her chest. "You have two minutes to give us the condensed version."

Karmen and Alice stared me down, and I had nowhere to run. Pipe was outside, and that was the last place I wanted to be. I sighed and slid the case of beer toward me. "It was nothing. Well, at least to Pipe it was nothing."

"Did he say that?" Alice asked.

"No, but I know that's how he feels."

Karmen grabbed my hand and squeezed it. "Nikki, you haven't seen him the past month. He hasn't been the same."

I shook her off and grabbed the case of beer. "Well, you may say that, but you didn't see what I did. I know Pipe is not interested in me for more than what he already got."

"Did you see him at the club with a girl? They hang around the common room like flies. I'm sure what you saw was nothing more than them trying to move up from a hang around to something more." Karmen had been around the club for a while now and knew more of the going ons than I did, but I know what I saw.

"It wasn't in the common room." I opened the fridge and managed to squeeze in the third case of beer. Alice wasn't kidding when she said she didn't know what kind of beer to get.

"So where was it?"

"I don't want to talk about this," I mumbled into the open fridge. I relived that shitty night enough on my own. I didn't need Karmen and Alice's commentary on it.

"That's fine. I'll just go ask Pipe."

Alice gasped, and I spun around. "You wouldn't dare."

Karmen shrugged and pulled a piece of licorice from the bag. "Try me."

I tossed my hands up in the air. "Fine. We had sex. Great sex. The best I've ever had in my life."

"Now we're talking." Alice pulled a chair out from the kitchen table and plopped down. "How did you go from the best sex of your life to he wants nothing to do with you?"

I ran my fingers through my hair. "Because it must have been only good for me because I went to his door a couple of weeks later and he was with another chick." Jesus. Those words hurt coming out.

"Shut up. You're kidding me. Why the hell wouldn't he want you again?"

I laughed and dropped my arm to my side. "Thanks for the vote of confidence, Alice."

"That can't be right, Nikki."

"I'm pretty sure she would know the difference between Pipe being with a chick or not." Thank goodness for Alice. I didn't want to tell Karmen about Pipe because she was dating his best friend and she might side with Pipe. Which is exactly what she was doing.

"I'm pretty sure she called him sugar plum, Karmen. So yeah, he was with another chick."

She shook her head and waved her hand at me. "That's not what I mean. I believe he was with another chick. He's a dick." Alice cackled, and I couldn't help but smile.

"Thank God you are back on Nikki's side. I thought you had defaulted to the dick's side."

"He's a dick, but I know h—"

"Baby girl," Nickel called from the doorway.

Karmen and Alice had been so into finding out what had happened between Pipe and me, I had completely forgotten to keep watch for the guys coming back in.

Karmen spun around and crossed her arms over her chest. "Sup, dude?"

Jesus. Karmen was so great at acting casual.

"Dude?" Nickel laughed.

Alice snorted and clapped her hand over her mouth. "Ignore that," she mumbled.

I shook my head. "That shit is not ignorable."

"You guys done talking about Pipe, or should we stay outside longer?"

My face heated, and I knew my cheeks were bright red. How the hell did he know we were talking about Pipe? "We were just talking about which movie to watch," I blurted.

Nickel gave me a knowing smile. "Sure."

Son of a damn monkey's uncle.

"How did you know we were talking about Pipe?" Alice asked.

Karmen kicked the leg of Alice's chair and shook her head. "Admit nothing," she said through clenched teeth.

Nickel hitched his thumb toward the window. "It's open, doll."

Ugh. I had opened it before Alice had picked me up because it was supposed to be a cooler night and I was looking forward to sleeping without having the A/C blowing on me.

"How much did you guys hear?" Karmen asked.

"Enough to know Pipe is a fucking idiot."

Hmm, well, it was nice to know Nickel thought what Pipe had done was dickish.

Karmen plastered a smile on her face and trotted over to Nickel. "You may enter, although I'm not sure Pipe is allowed to come in."

Nickel wrapped his arms around Karmen's waist and pressed a kiss to her lips. "Easy, tiger. It's not any of our business."

Karmen growled.

"It's in the past, guys. Don't make a big deal about it, okay?" It was bad enough everyone knew I was dumb enough to sleep with Pipe, I didn't need to have Pipe know it still bothered me. I saw movement behind Nickel and knew Pipe was coming.

Nickel's eyes connected with mine. "I don't think he heard."

Well, that was a bit of relief.

Alice jumped up from her chair and started ripping everything out of the bags.

Nickel moved to the side with Karmen in his arms, and Pipe walked into my duplex.

My duplex I thought was rather spacious, and one of the nicer places I had lived. That is, until Pipe stepped through the doorway and it felt like the room was closing in on me, and all of my things I had bought seemed dingy and shitty.

Hell, this man messed with my head.

"I'll get the snacks ready if you want to get the movie going." Alice threw me a look that screamed *get it together*. I must have looked like some pathetic puppy whose bone had gotten taken away.

"Uh, I'll, well…" What the hell was going on? I was having a brain meltdown in the middle of my kitchen.

How did I get here?

Karmen wrapped up in Nickel's arms, Pipe standing next to my couch from the local thrift shop, and Alice in a cow print onesie pulling every snack imaginable out of plastic bags.

"Nikki, movie, now," Karmen prompted me.

My eyes darted to her, and I slightly shook my head.

I was lame with a capital L because I couldn't remember where the movies were. Hell, I couldn't remember my own name at the moment.

"I know, I'll get the snacks, Karmen can get the movie from on top of the TV that I rented, and Nikki can run to the bathroom to freshen up." Alice stood in front of me and put her hands on my shoulders. "I'll help her to the bathroom." She pushed me to the side, and I stumbled down the short hallway that lead to the bathroom and two bedrooms.

She reached around me, pushed open the bathroom, and pushed me in. "Get it together, woman. You have five minutes to walk out of this bathroom and act like that hunk of a gorgeous man has no effect on you." She flipped on the light, stepped back, and slammed the door shut. "Get it together, Nikki," she called.

I face-planted against the door and closed my eyes. That was way easier said than done.

How do you act like your world wasn't changed after one kiss?

How do you ignore your feelings?

How do you ignore Pipe Marks?

I had all the questions, but none of the answers.

I was so screwed.

*

Pipe

"You sure you shouldn't maybe go check on her?"

Karmen looked over her shoulder down the hallway. "I'm sure she'll be out any minute. Just watch the movie," she tsked at Nickel.

I kicked back in the recliner and took a sip of my beer. Alice had marched Nikki into the bathroom over ten minutes ago, and she had yet to surface.

"Maybe she decided to put her pajamas on. Lord knows I'm comfy as hell. I don't know why everyone doesn't wear their pajamas all of the time." Alice was laid out on the floor with three pillows behind her back, and I couldn't help but think she looked like roadkill on the floor. I had to wonder how many cows had given their lives in the name of her pajamas. Alice shoved a handful of popcorn in her mouth and looked up at me. "Or, she's waiting for you to leave."

This was also a new development.

Alice hated me and had no qualms about not hiding it.

"But you invited us over to watch a movie, Alice. I don't think it would be nice of me to leave." And to think I had initially liked Alice.

"I'm sure Nikki will understand you having to leave. I'm sure you have something better you could be doing right now." She snickered under her breath and shoved more popcorn into her mouth.

"Nowhere else I'd rather be right now," I mumbled. Except I wouldn't mind being in the bathroom with Nikki at this moment. Once I talked her into getting over whatever the hell was bugging her, I'd like to act out the fantasy I had with her in the shower.

"You wanna grab me another beer?" Nickel asked.

"Make Pipe get it," Karmen muttered. Her eyes were trained on the TV, and she was eating licorice like it was going out of style. She was sprawled out on Nickel's lap, and he was slowly rubbing her belly.

"I got it." I kicked down the footrest on the recliner and strolled into the kitchen.

Nikki's fridge was filled with every junk food imaginable, and the bottom was filled with beer. It was a bachelor's dream.

"Looking for something?"

I froze mid-reach and looked over my shoulder.

Nikki was standing behind me, clothes changed, and her hair flowing down her shoulders.

She was fucking gorgeous.

"Uh, I was just getting a beer."

She nodded and tugged on the hem of her shirt. "Okay."

We both stood there, staring at each other, speechless.

"Beer," Nickel called.

Nikki jumped and nodded at me. "I'll just, uh, go." She spun around, bumping into the table, and plopped into the chair I had been sitting in.

I grabbed two beers, popped the top on them, and handed one to Nickel.

"Thanks, brother."

I sat down in the small space left on the couch next to Karmen and Nickel and felt like a fat man trying to sit in a crib. "You think you two could share the fucking couch?" I bitched.

Karmen scooted closer to Nickel giving me about three more inches. "Better?"

Not really, but I wasn't about to get into it with a pregnant chick. "It'll do, doll." I could have laid on the floor by Alice, but I liked the fact I could watch Nikki without her knowing I was looking at her.

She had her legs tucked under her, and her eyes were trained on the TV. Her back was ramrod straight, and she looked tense as hell.

She never was like this with me before. All the times we had hung out before, she was carefree, saying and doing whatever she wanted. Don't even get me started on the night I had finally fallen into bed with her. I'm pretty sure Nickel wouldn't appreciate me sporting wood next to his woman.

My beer dangled from my fingertips, and while everyone else watched the movie, I was watching Nikki slowly relax into the chair. She leaned her head back, and a small smile played on her lips.

Alice had a running commentary about what was happening on the screen, and Nickel would tell her to put a sock in it every five minutes or so.

By the time the credits rolled, Karmen was fast asleep, my butt was numb, and I watched Nikki more than I did the movie.

"Should we watch another one?" Alice asked from the floor.

Nickel shook his head and slowly rolled Karmen off his arm. "I think I'm going to get sleeping beauty back to the hotel. First, I need to get feeling back to my arm though." He raised his arm over his head and shook his hand.

Karmen grunted and curled into Nickel. "I'm not moving. You go back to the hotel."

Nickel chuckled and ran his fingers through her hair. "I think you'll be more comfortable in bed, baby girl."

"I'm not moving."

"You said that already," Alice laughed.

"We have a hotel room, Karmen," Nickel insisted.

"Then go use it," she mumbled. "Give me a blanket, and my pregnant ass isn't moving until morning."

Nickel looked at me for help, but I didn't have a clue what to tell him. Could you really make a pregnant chick do anything she didn't want to? "Carry her?" Chicks dug being carried, didn't they?

"If you even try to move me from this couch, I'm naming our baby Beaufort and moving in with Nikki." Karmen opened one eye and looked over at me. "Try it, ass."

I held up my hands and shook my head. "I have no plans of touching you, darlin'. I'm more than okay with going back to the hotel by myself."

"I'm sure you are," she scowled. "No skanks in my bed, Pipe."

What the hell was she talking about? I couldn't remember the last time I had been with a chick. The only stranger who I had been within the past month was my left hand. Jacking off with your hand that wasn't dominate mimicked the feel of someone else jerking you off. The things you learn on the ol' interwebs. Plus, free porn. "How is it your bed if you ain't sleeping in it?"

She closed her eye and smiled. "Because Nickel paid for that room, so both of those beds are mine as far as I'm concerned."

"Then get your ass up and go lay in *both* of your beds." Damn sassy tonight.

"No, you can have the bed. I'm staying here."

I looked up at Nickel. "Your woman is damn looney, brother."

"She's Karmen."

Karmen raised her head and leveled her gaze on Nickel. "I'm not sure what you mean by that answer. I'm torn between being offended and kissing you."

"Kiss me and don't think about it."

"No, I think I'm going with offended." She laid her head back down and pointed at the door. "You and Pipe can be bed buddies. I'm staying here with Nikki and Alice. We're gonna have a slumber party and talk about boys."

"Hell yes," Alice shouted as she shot up from the floor. "Once these two leave, we can make a blanket cave on the couch, bring out more snacks, and watch more Vin."

Karmen moved her hand to point at Alice. "What she said. Although, we're also going to talk about your somewhat unhealthy obsession with Vin. You do know he's real, but not *real*, right?"

Alice tilted her head to the side. "I don't think I like the way you are talking right now. Next, you are going to tell me book boyfriends aren't real. And if that's the truth, I don't think I want to live in that world."

Nickel scooted away from Karmen and moved to the door. "I don't know what the hell is going on right now. I'm going to the hotel. You coming with me or not, woman?"

"No. Take Pipe. You two can snuggle. Come back over in the morning for breakfast. Actually, make it brunch. I need my sleep."

"Don't you think maybe you should run this impromptu sleepover by Nikki before you plan it?"

"She can stay," Nikki piped up. "I really don't mind."

Nickel growled but knew he was outnumbered and there was no way he was going to be able to talk Karmen into going back to the hotel with him. It was three against one, and I had no plans on joining Nickel's side because I didn't want these three against me.

"I'm not leaving you with the car."

Karmen laughed and sat up.

I stood up and grabbed my empty can from the side table.

"I just pictured you on the back of Pipe's bike." Karmen cackled and howled, hitting the couch.

Nickel tossed his arms up in the air. "I'm done with you tonight," he growled. "I love you, baby girl, but I think Pipe might be right about you being a little looney."

Karmen tossed one of the throw pillows at Nickel's retreating back before he ducked out the front door.

"I love you too, ass," she called.

"I know you love my ass, baby girl." The door slammed shut behind him, and Karmen turned her glare on me.

"Behave."

Whatever the hell that meant. What did she think Nickel and I were going to do? The only plan I had was to grab one of the cases of beer from the fridge, toss it in Nickel's car before he left, then drink back at the hotel. "That's all I do, darlin'."

Karmen rolled her eyes and tossed the other throw pillow at me. "You don't even know the definition of behaving."

"Pfft, now that's the truth," Nikki mumbled.

She had barely said a word during the movie, and now the first thing she says is she agrees I don't know how to behave.

I grabbed a case of beer from the fridge, gave a two-finger salute to the ladies, and made my way out the door. No matter what I tried to do tonight, I knew it wasn't going to be enough.

"Make sure you lock the door," Nickel called before I slammed it shut.

I handed him the beer and pulled a cigarette from my pocket. "I'm not sure what the hell that was, but I know me leaving was the best decision."

Nickel tossed the beer on the passenger seat and slipped into the driver's seat. "Damn woman. It's a good thing I love her sass and she's carrying my kid."

"Pretty sure you love everything about her, brother. Otherwise you wouldn't put up with any of that shit."

"Now that's the truth," Nickel mumbled. "I'm gonna head to the hotel. You coming back right away?"

I lit the end of my cigarette and inhaled deeply. "I'll be right behind you," I exhaled.

Nickel cranked up the car, backed out of the driveway, and headed down the road.

I leaned against my bike, looking up at Nikki's duplex.

It was pretty nice.

Nicer than any place I had lived before.

Hell, more than half of my life I had lived in one of the rooms at the club.

I spotted a "for rent" sign on the other half of the duplex, and an idea formed in my head faster than I could finish my cigarette.

I still had no idea what the hell was going on with Nikki and me, but I was damn determined to figure it out.

Tomorrow was going to be the first day of my harebrained scheme and it was hopefully going to settle whatever the hell was going on with us.

At least, that was what I hoped was going to happen.

*

Chapter 7

Nikki

"I thought you were tired?"

Karmen glanced over her shoulder at me and opened the fridge. "I was. Then I took a nap. Now I'm good to go for at least another hour."

"You're going to give Nickel gray hair." I grabbed the remote from the end table and put on the local news.

"Hey, I thought we were going to watch another movie," Alice protested. She had a bag of chips sitting next to her and a container of dip in her hand. After the guys left, Alice raided the fridge and had taken claim of half of the couch.

"I can't do it, Alice. I can't watch those damn movies anymore. I'm starting to go crazy and have dreams of Vin taking me away in his fast car."

Karmen closed the fridge and pointed her bottle of water at Alice. "You know, there's something not right in your head with all this Vin talk." Hell, leave it to Karmen to get right to the point. "Like, honey, you had two living, breathing hunks of men with you tonight, and you only had eyes for a guy on the TV you will never meet."

Alice rolled her eyes and loaded a chip up with dip. "Those two guys are very much taken by you guys. I'm not going to drool over them when they have zero interest in me."

Karmen cracked open her water and shook her head. "So, Vin is a much better option for you?" She took a sip then slammed her bottle down on the counter. "We should go back to the bar. We can find you a guy."

Alice cackled uncontrollably, and I couldn't help but smile at Karmen. She really had no clue.

When Alice had first told me the dating pool was nonexistent in Kales Corners, I hadn't believed her. After spending a week in town, I fully understood what she meant.

If you weren't hooked up and dating someone by freshman year, you were the odd man out. Well, there were people still single, but Alice had no interest in them. I had first thought she was just picky, but after meeting the four men in Kales that were available, I had to agree with her, they weren't the right guy.

"You know when we went to the bar, and Nikki and I were the only ones there when you guys walked in?" Karmen nodded her head. "Well, I can guarantee you The Bar is now closed because there is no way in hell they were going to keep the lights on for no one but the bartender."

Karmen rolled her eyes and grabbed the half-eaten bag of licorice off the counter. "I don't believe you."

I had sounded just like Karmen a month ago.

Alice grinned and pulled her phone out of her pocket. She swiped left and right a couple of times then held her phone out to Karmen. "They're closed. They posted on their Facebook page."

Karmen grabbed the phone from her hand. "Well, I'm a monkey's uncle. You're right." Karmen flipped the phone around so I could see.

I nodded and turned back to the TV. "I believed her. Even though that was my first visit to The Bar, I know there aren't enough people in this town to keep it open."

Karmen handed the phone back to Alice and plopped down on the couch next to her. "Sorry. I totally get this is a small town, but I figured with it being a small town everyone would be at The Bar drinking because there wasn't anything else to do."

"There normally are about four guys who shut the bar down every night, but Alice's mom made lasagna or some bullshit, so they all left."

Karmen popped a chip into her mouth and crunched down on it. "Well, since there isn't anywhere else to go, and all the movies you have you guys watched fifty times, I guess the only thing left to do is talk about Nikki and Pipe."

Alice high-fived Karmen. "Best idea I have heard all night," she sang. She rubbed her hands together and dug another chip out of the bag. "I feel that there is more than what she told us before."

Karmen scoffed. "Please, I doubt she even scraped the surface on all the sexual tension between them."

I sat down in the recliner and kicked my feet up. "There isn't anything else to tell. We had flirted, had sex, flirted some more, and then it was over."

"You see, the way I look at it, if all he wanted was sex, then why did he flirt with you after you guys had sex? That don't make sense," Karmen insisted.

I looked over and shook my head. "It makes sense because he is a man, and they don't make sense."

Alice stopped mid-chew and tilted her head. "I don't know if what either of you just said makes sense."

It made sense. At least what I said. I knew the score when I had hooked up with Pipe, but like every dumb woman who sets their sights on an unattainable man, they think they can change them. I was the latest dumb woman in a long line. "It makes sense, because Pipe got exactly what he wanted from me, and then he was on to the next woman."

"I don't think that's entirely true. I think you confused the hell out of Pipe, and he had no clue what to do, so he just did what he always used to do."

"Be a man," Alice and I sang out in unison.

Karmen sat back and rubbed her belly. "I still don't entirely understand why you ran away, though. I know you always talked about leaving Weston, but girl, you just left like a thief in the night. You were there, and then you were gone." Her tone was sad and hurt, and I was the reason for that.

I sighed and closed my eyes. "I'm sorry I took off so quickly. I just needed to get gone."

"But why couldn't you have talked to me? I would have understood."

"You would have understood that a man I had no connection to other than one night and some flirting with hurt me to the point where I didn't even want to be in the same town as him?" I squeezed my eyes shut tight, fighting off the tears that were threatening to fall.

"Oh hell, Nikki. Don't make me cry. Nickel says I'm a blubbering mess, and I'm starting to believe him. This baby has me all out of whack." I heard Karmen sniffle, and I cracked open one eye to see her wipe her nose with the back of her hand. "You should have talked to me, woman. We would have figured out how to get Pipe together."

"That's the thing, Kar, I didn't want to have to convince him to be with me. You can't force someone to feel the same way you do. He didn't want me again, so he found something he did want. Too bad for me, I wasn't what he wanted." I hated having to say that out loud. Pipe had cut me deep. The way I felt when I was even in the same room with him was something had never experienced before. After Pipe and I had slept together, everything changed for me. I had never felt a pull to a man like I did with Pipe. For a bit, I thought he had felt the same way. We flirted, brushed up against each other to feel each other again, and I thought I saw a promise of something more whenever he looked at me.

I guess I read everything wrong, because by the time I worked up enough courage to go to him, he had moved on, and was left with a broken heart and felt like a complete fool. Who reads a man that wrong? In my head we were basically married, and in his, I was just another notch on his bedpost.

Fool.

"Pipe is such an idiot," Karmen sobbed.

Alice had a look of terror on her face as she watched Karmen grab a handful of chips and shove them into her mouth while she sobbed.

"Did Pipe break up with you or Nikki?" she asked.

"I am Nikki," Karmen babbled. "When she hurts, so do I. She's like my sister."

Alice slowly turned her head to look at me and grimaced. "I'm not sure what to do," she whispered. "I feel like she can flip on me at any minute."

"She can hear you," I whispered back, laughing.

She turned back to Karmen and plastered a smile on her face. "I'm sorry for your loss."

Karmen stopped crying, and now it was her turn to look at me. "Huh?" she asked, confused.

Alice shrugged her shoulders. "I felt that was a safe thing to say. Can you really attack someone who says sorry?"

Her reasoning was good. "True. Plus, you confused the hell out of her too. Apologize and blind her with confusion."

Karmen shot up and grabbed a paper towel off of the counter. "I'm not attacking anyone," she sniffled. "I'm just a little emotional, and I know Nikki is hurting even though she plays it off."

"I'm fine, Karmen. And soon, I'll be good. I just needed to get out of Weston." Everything about that damn town seemed to remind me of Pipe. Even things that had nothing to do with him reminded me of him because I would think of going to places with him or doing things with him. I was a mess when it came to the man, and the only way to get over Pipe was to completely get away.

"But why do you have to go so far away from me? We've been together since we were kids, and now you're just gone." She was on the verge of tears again.

Sweet heavens. Talking to her really was like walking through a minefield. One wrong word, and kablooey, she was crying and losing it.

She looked down at her belly and glared at it. "How is it possible to love and hate this kid all at the same time? What in the hell is going on with me?"

"At least she knows she's unstable," Alice mumbled.

Jesus. "Not helping, Alice," I hissed. I snapped down the footrest, rocked out of my chair, and wrapped my arms around Karmen. "You need to breathe, Karmen."

"I am breathing," she insisted. "Although I'm apparently unstable." She pulled out of my arms and leveled her glare on Alice.

Alice held up her hands. "I'm sorry for your loss."

Karmen dropped her arms to her side. "I don't even know what to say to that." She turned to look at me. "This is my replacement?"

I ran my fingers through my hair. "Well..."

Karmen stomped her foot. "Seriously? You were replacing me?" She looked outraged and ready to flip the switch and go crazy on me.

I laughed. There wasn't anything else to do. This baby really was causing havoc to her hormones. "She's not your replacement, Kar. I could never replace your crazy ass."

"Yeah. I mean, you totally have the market cornered on being the pregnant, crazy, dating a biker, friend. That is all you, sister." Alice pointed her finger at Karmen and winked. "No one can pull that off like you do."

"You know, I thought she was super sweet when I first met her, but it's like the more comfortable she gets, the more sarcastic she gets." Karmen flopped back down on the couch and grabbed the bag of chips from Alice.

"See, that's my niche. The quiet, shy, yet terribly sarcastic one." She wiped her hands on her legs and nodded at the TV. "So, you think we can watch something other than the news? I'm more informed on what's going on around here than they are."

"Only if I get to pick the movie," I insisted.

Alice rolled her eyes but agreed.

"Hold on. We never finished our conversation." Karmen rubbed her belly and leveled her gaze on me. "Are you ever going to move back to Weston, and am I still your best friend?"

I rolled my eyes and shook my head. "This is home for now, and I can't even imagine ever replacing you."

Karmen sighed and shoved a chip into her mouth. "I guess I'll accept those answers for now. I at least know where you live now so I can just visit you whenever I want. Maybe I could ask Nickel to move the club here."

"Wow, he's the president?" Alice asked.

Karmen laughed and shook her head. "No, he's the Sergeant at Arms. I just like to think he could talk Wrecker and Pipe into moving," she giggled.

"I think that is one idea you just need to give up on." I grabbed a movie from the pile in the cabinet under the TV and slipped it into the Blu Ray player. "I think Kales Corners is a bit behind the times for the Fallen Lords."

"This is true," Karmen laughed. "I don't think they could handle one bar and limited, well, everything."

I sat back down and pointed the remote at the TV. "Okay, so are we all done talking about me?"

"For now," Karmen and Alice said in unison.

I hit play and kicked up the footrest of the recliner. "Good. Now we can watch my favorite movie ever. Renee Zellweger and Harry Connick Jr. in the freakin' hilarious *New in Town*. Prepare to laugh your ass off, ladies."

"Oh geez. I've seen this five times with you, woman," Karmen laughed.

"But you know you're going to laugh still."

"Again, this is true," she agreed.

"Hmm, I've never seen this before," Alice hummed.

"Probably because it doesn't have Vin in it," Karmen snickered.

"Hey, I'm the snarky friend in this relationship," Alice grabbed the bag of chips back from Karmen and tucked it next to her side. "We all have our roles. Stick to 'em."

"Is she for real?" Karmen asked.

Unfortunately, she was. Karmen was right when she said Alice started out shy and quiet then once she got comfortable enough, she cranked up the sarcasm and lost any filter she had before. "She most definitely is."

Karmen settled back into the couch, kicked her feet up between her and Alice, and ignored the glared Alice gave her. "I'm the needy, crazy, pregnant one. Don't mess with me," Karmen reminded her.

And that was how we watched my favorite movie.

My crazy pregnant friend annoying the hell out of my new sarcastic friend all while I tried not to think about Pipe or how much my heart still hurt when I was around him.

The man had broken my heart, but I still wanted him, nonetheless.

I really was a fool.

*

Chapter 8

Pipe

"Who the hell were you on the phone with? It's barely nine o'clock in the morning."

"A realtor."

Nickel raised his head from the pillow and cracked one eye open. "Say that again?"

I shook my head and walked into the tiny hotel bathroom. It was a good thing Karmen hadn't slept at the hotel with us last night. This room barely squeezed in the two double beds leaving two feet between the TV and bed. Shit was fucking tight. "I was on the phone with a realtor," I called. I turned on the water and splashed cold water on my face. I had woken up twenty minutes ago, immediately grabbed my phone, and headed outside to put my plan into motion.

"Okay, so I did hear you correctly," Nickel mumbled.

I grabbed one of the dingy towels and wiped my face. "Yeah," I mumbled.

"So, you buying a house in Weston?"

I leaned against the door frame and shook my head. "Nah. I'm renting a place."

"Really? You're done living at the club? I never thought I would see the day."

I shrugged and tossed the towel over my shoulder. "Guess I'm finally growing up."

"So what place are you renting? Please don't say one of those shit ass apartments over in Clearview."

"Nah, it's a duplex."

Nickel scratched his head and fell back on his pillow. "Where the hell is that?"

"About five minutes from here."

Nickel shot up. "Hold the fuck up. You're moving here? How the hell is that going to work with the club?"

"I already talked to Wrecker. I don't plan on living here longer than six months. We're only an hour from Weston, so it's really not an issue for me to drive back and forth every day."

"You're fucking crazy, brother. You know that chick intentionally moved away from you, right? Now you're going to chase her down and move in directly next door to her? Seems a bit drastic to me."

"I think you mean crazy." I still couldn't believe myself that I was doing this. Seeing Nikki had fucked me.

When she was in Weston, living in the same town as me, I didn't feel rushed. I knew she was different from any chick I had been with, but I figured I had time. Now with her gone and possibly moving on from whatever the hell happened to us, it lit a fire under my ass. I still didn't know what I wanted, but I knew I wasn't going to give her up that easily.

"So, what? You gonna move in next to her and just happen to fall into her bed every night? I have to tell you, brother, Nikki is nothing like the chicks in your past. Which, by the way, was exactly what you treated her like back in Weston."

"What the hell do you mean?" There was no way Nickel knew what happened between Nikki and me.

"I mean the fact she walked in on you getting it on with some club whore."

"You fucking spying on me, asshole?"

Nickel shook his head. "No. She told Karmen and Alice what happened between you two, and I happened to overhear."

"What the hell did she say?"

Nickel shrugged and tossed his feet over the edge of the bed. "She came over to your room, planning on hooking up with you and you were there with some other chick."

"That's all she said?"

"Wasn't what she said, more like how she said it. You should have known that although she said she knew the score with you, she wasn't going to be able to be pushed away."

I ran my fingers through my hair. I would need a fucking cigarette if I was going to have this conversation. "I didn't push her away. I wasn't fucking thinking when Toni said she could come to my room."

"Obviously, since you decided Toni was a better choice than Nikki."

Toni was far from better than Nikki. All Toni was good for was relieving the pressure a bit. "Look, I fucked up. A guy like me never gets a shot at a chick like Nikki. I live in a world of Toni's who are a dime a dozen and disposable."

"Well, you're a fucking idiot for not realizing soon enough Nikki was better than your wham, bam, thank you ma'am bullshit."

"Look, I don't need you to go all fucking Dr. Phil on me. I fucked up, and I'm going to try to fix it."

"Well, good luck brother, because from what I saw and heard from Nikki, you got a lot of fucking work in front of you for her to even start talking to you again, let alone letting you back into her bed."

I walked back into the bathroom and tossed the towel on the floor.

I may have a lot of work to do, but I was hoping the reward at the end was going to be worth it.

Nikki was going to be my reward.

*

Nikki

"I'll call you when we get back to the club. I have work all week, but Nickel said we can come back out next weekend to hang out."

"You're welcome to come whenever you want. Maybe next time you could bring Cora with you and leave the guys at home."

Karmen glanced over her shoulder at Nickel who was standing next to Pipe and his bike. "I think I can make that happen. I'm pretty sure if Cora was with me, Nickel wouldn't have a problem. She's one tough chick who could take care of me," she laughed.

"No plotting, woman," Nickel called as he pointed his finger at us.

"That man has no idea what he signed up for," I mumbled.

"Trust me, he had an idea, but there's still more to come," Karmen cackled.

She wrapped her arms around me and pulled me into a tight hug. "No crying," I warned.

"I'm not crying," she mumbled into my neck. "I have something in my eye."

"Is that what you're going with?"

She pulled away and shrugged. "Just go with it. The only reason I'm not kidnapping you and tossing you in the truck is because I know I'll see you a few days."

"Well, thank you for that." There was the crazy part coming out.

"Make sure you tell Alice bye for me. She's really not that bad. Not a replacement for me, but she'll keep an eye on you for me when I can't be here."

I laughed and leaned against the porch rail. "Well, I'm glad you can see a use for her. I've become rather fond of her. She's one of the first people I met when I moved to town."

Karmen wagged her finger in my face. "Just don't replace me, woman."

I held up my hand. "Not gonna happen, okay?"

"Baby girl, let's get a move on. I got shit to do. You being one of them."

Karmen rolled her eyes and gave me another quick hug. "It's probably a good thing you and Pipe didn't work. You'd be putting up with stuff like that."

I plastered a smile on my face and nodded my head. "Yeah, thank God."

Karmen shook her head. "Nice try. Maybe next week, you'll be better at faking being okay."

"Give me a little credit. The man is standing right there looking like every girl's wet dream." Pipe was smoking again, and I wished I was his cigarette.

Damn. They needed to leave, like now.

"I'll call you. Make sure you answer the damn phone," Karmen called.

Nickel grabbed her hand and pulled her to the car. He tucked her into the passenger side and gave me a two-finger flick before he slid into the driver's side.

Nickel backed out the driveway, and Pipe sat on his bike watching me.

What did he want? I wasn't going to say bye to him.

I couldn't put myself through that.

I stood my ground on the porch, gave him a little wave, then disappeared into the house. I slammed the door shut behind me, giving myself credit for not giving into my need to go to him.

I couldn't control myself not to peek through the curtains and watch him, though.

God broke the mold when he made Pipe Marks. Tall, powerful build. Strong, broad shoulders. Dark hair, long enough to give him the wild, carefree look. Chiseled features that made my knees weak. Tattoos covering skin that screamed bad ass.

He was fucking hot, and there wasn't any way I could deny it.

He cranked up his bike, gave one last look at my duplex, and took off down the street.

That was going to be the last time I saw Pipe.

I couldn't go through this one more time. He broke my heart all over again.

Pipe was gone, and I was going to be okay.
Eventually.

*

Chapter 9

Pipe

"You sure about this?"

I tossed three more shirts in my bag and zipped it shut. "What's the sense in waiting?"

Wrecker kicked back in the chair I had in the corner. "You think about the possibility this chick left because she really doesn't want to see you again?"

It had crossed my mind. "Doesn't matter."

"You bump your head while you were in Kales Corners? What the hell do you mean it doesn't matter?"

I tossed my bag over my shoulder and grabbed my cut off the bed. "It means if she doesn't want me there, then I'll have to change her mind." How the hell I was going to do that I had no idea, but I knew I had to give it a shot.

"So you just move in next door to her, woo her or some shit, and then you both move back here happily ever after?" Wrecker scoffed and shook his head. "You sure you ain't drunk right now? Because that is the stupidest idea I've ever heard."

"You didn't say that shit when I asked what you thought of me moving to Kales Corners."

Wrecker stood up and stroked his beard. "That's because I thought you were moving in with the damn chick because she wanted you to. Crazy fucker, moving for a chick that doesn't want you anymore."

That right there, I didn't believe. Nikki may have barely spoken a word to me, but I saw the way she looked at me when she thought I wasn't paying attention. What cemented the idea of me moving there was when I saw her watching me from the window. If she didn't care about me, she wouldn't have done that.

"You're just gonna have to trust me about this, brother."

"Well, you're your own man. All I can tell you is you're fucking crazy."

I may be, but I didn't know what else to do. The chick had somehow managed to get under my skin, and I had no fucking clue how to get over her. So, I might as well try to get under her again and either work her out of my system or just make her fucking mine.

*

Chapter 10

Nikki

"Where is my hash?"

Bos leveled his stare at me. "You write it on the ticket?"

Not this again. "I gave you a separate ticket for it."

"Then it'll be coming."

"I put down that it was supposed to go with the ticket before it. How would you like to be sitting at a table where everyone else gets their food, and you don't?"

"That wouldn't happen because I know to put everything on one ticket." He moved away from the window and grabbed a pan off the heat. "One table, one ticket," he reminded me.

"You know what, Bos, just make the damn hash." Gah, I was so ready to go home. It was a quarter to seven, and I had just over an hour left until we closed.

"I'm making it, I'm making it," he grumbled.

Alice had the night off, and I was the only one working beside Bos. The grumpy old man was not the greatest company.

"Hash up," he shouted as he smashed the bell that was next to my head.

I glared at Bos and snatched the plate off of the ledge. "I know where you live, old man."

"That mean you're going to stop by and clip my toenails for me?"

I wrinkled my nose and shook my head. "Why in the hell would you think that?"

"Because that's all I need from you, darlin'. Mazie takes care of all of my other needs." He wiggled his eyebrows, and from the way he moved, it looked like he was trying to do a two-step shimmy.

I gulped and closed my eyes. "Jesus, Bos, I'm never going to be able to wipe that from my mind."

"That ol' Mazie could teach you young guns a thing or two."

While I headed over to the table at the far end of the restaurant with their hash, I tried to imagine what Mazie could teach me. Except I was picturing Bos on the receiving end.

Sweet Jesus. That was not pretty.

"Here ya go," I mumbled as I set the plate down. "Is there anything else I can get for you?"

"Um, I think I'm good, Nikki, but there is a question I have." Richard shifted uncomfortably in the booth and ducked his head.

"What's up?" I chirped. Richard came in every Monday and Wednesday like clockwork. He sat in the same booth and ordered the same thing. Except for today, he had added on the hash last minute. I was rather shocked when he had called me over to add it to his usual.

"I uh, I was, well, I was wondering if you were seeing anyone." His cheeks flushed deep red, and his eyes were still pointed down at his lap.

"Well, not really. Not since I moved to Kales Corners. I've been kind of busy just settling in and working." I knew where this was headed, and I was scrambling trying to figure out how I was going to let him down easy without hurting his feelings.

"Well, you're doing a really good job here. Way better than Alice ever did."

I hesitantly smiled at his compliment. Putting down Alice wasn't really a wise choice. "Alice taught me everything she knows. I would be a mess without her taking me under her wing." When I had decided to apply at the diner for work, Alice had been my saving grace. Bos had been the one to interview me, and I could tell he had written me off the second I told him who I was. Alice had bustled out of the kitchen, tying her apron behind her back and told Bos to cut the bullshit and give me the job.

Back in Weston, Karmen and I had worked at the nursing home, but I knew I wouldn't be able to work at another place like that without

Karmen. We were a team, and as much I told myself moving here was the best choice, I still missed her something fierce.

Richard cleared his throat, knocking me out of my thoughts. "So, I was wondering if maybe we could go to the movies Friday and see a movie at the movie theater.?"

I couldn't help but smile at his bumbling. Richard was a nice guy, and only a few years older than me, but he really wasn't my type. Thankfully, I didn't need to make up an excuse why I couldn't go out with him. "Actually, my best friend from Weston is coming over Friday and staying with me all weekend."

"Oh," he mumbled. "Maybe we can do it some other time."

"Yeah, maybe we can." There, I didn't crush his hopes, but I also didn't agree I would go out with him. "I'll let you get back to eating before your food gets cold. Make sure you tell me how that hash is before you leave. Bos makes some of the best."

Richard nodded and tucked into eating.

I moseyed back to the register, wiping down tables as I went.

"Heard you got a date for Friday," Bos said quietly.

I rolled my eyes and slapped my rag down on the counter. "You might not want to eavesdrop, Bos. You might hear something you don't like."

He rolled his eyes and leaned against the pass thru window. "Just be careful with Richard. He's a nice guy, but he's a bit strange."

"What does that mean?" I glanced over at Richard, and he looked like your normal, average guy. "Does he have six toes or something?"

Bos shook his head. "No, not that crazy. I mean his marbles aren't all where they are supposed to be. He's always been a strange one, but I've heard some not so nice things from the women he manages to get dates with."

"Well, dang, Bos. It sounds like you actually care about me."

"Don't read too much into, darlin'. I just don't want to have to read your obit in the newspaper and have to find a new waitress. Stay away from Richard," he warned.

I saluted him and grabbed my rag off the counter. "Can do, because I had no plans on dating him anyway. But your overwhelming concern for me has truly touched my heart."

Bos flipped me off and lumbered over to the storage closet mumbling about smart asses and women who are full of piss and vinegar.

"I'll take that as a compliment," I hollered to his back.

After Richard finished his meal, he left me a huge tip which I regretfully pocketed, then Bos and I closed the doors and cleaned up.

"What are you doing?" I asked as Bos followed me closely out the door and grabbed my arm to keep me close to him as he locked the door with his other hand.

"Just humor me, young gun."

"Young gun?" I scoffed. What in the hell was this man up to?

"I know you didn't notice, but I have for a while. I was hoping he was harmless, but tonight cemented my thoughts. Richard is after you."

"After me? What in the world do you mean?"

"I mean, I don't have a good feeling about him. I'm walking you to your car, and then I'm going to follow you home."

I batted my eyelashes and fanned myself with my hand. "Well I do declare, Bos, I thought you had Mazie to take care of all your primal needs."

"Fucking smartass," he mumbled. "Just humor an old man, okay?"

"Whatever you say, Bos." If it made him feel better to follow me home, then so be it.

"How much of a tip did he leave?" he asked as I unlocked my car doors.

I glanced over my shoulder or him and gulped. "Fifteen."

He ran his fingers through his thinning hair. "Nikki, his damn meal didn't cost more than ten dollars. You don't think it's odd that he left you a hundred and fifty percent tip?"

"I don't know, Bos. I guess I didn't really think about it." I looked around nervously. "You don't think he's watching us right now, do you?" Now I was freaked the hell out.

Bos shook his head. "I saw him take off. You're good right now. I don't think he's going to do anything, Nikki, but you need to just keep your head up."

He opened my door for me and glanced over his shoulder. "Where are you parked?"

"Out back."

Now that Bos had freaked the fuck out of me, there was no way in hell I was going to let him out of my sight. "Well, hop in, and I'll give you a ride to it."

Bos rounded the car, and I slid into the driver's seat. "So, are you going to tell me crazy stuff you heard about Richard?" I slowly drove around the restaurant and stopped next to Bos' beat up Oldsmobile.

"It's nothing I've actually seen myself, but it's just when he gets attached to a chick, he becomes obsessed with her."

I slowly turned my head to look at him. "Gee, that makes me feel so much better. He asked me out, and I told him I had plans this weekend."

Bos patted my shoulder and opened the door. "I'm sure it's nothing, but I just thought you should have a little heads up. Don't stress out over it."

"Bos, you scared the living shit out of me."

He chuckled and shook his head. "That's not what I meant to do. Look, I'll follow you home, and you'll be fine. Everything I've heard could just be rumors."

I took a deep breath and nodded my head. "Okay, I'll put my freak out on hold for the time being. He seemed fine when I told him I was busy." This was Richard we were talking about. I had never gotten the vibe from him that he was a psycho. I was going to be fine. I just needed to keep repeating that over and over until I believed it.

Bos gave me a reassuring smile. He slammed my door shut, got into his car, and motioned for me to go.

Only I could move to a new town and get a creepy admirer who might want to make a meat-suit out of me.

The five-minute drive to my duplex felt like it took forever, but I finally made it home, and everything looked normal.

Well, except for the fact the "for rent" sign in the yard of the other side of the duplex was gone, and there was light in all of the windows.

I pulled into the driveway, and Bos pulled in behind me.

"Looks like you've finally got a neighbor," he called from his open window.

"Yeah, I guess so." It had been nice the past month not having anyone directly next to me. Now it looked like I was going to have to be neighborly. There wasn't a car in the driveway, but they might have parked in the garage. "You hear anything about someone moving in?"

He shook his head. "Not a word. Although Mazie hasn't been over in a couple of days, and she's who I get all my gossip from."

I held up my hand. "Stop right there. I don't want to know any more about Mazie." Dirty old man.

Bos chuckled and shifted his car into reverse. "Get in the house so I can head on home and wait for Mazie."

"Say no more!" I jogged up the front steps, stabbed my key into the lock, and pushed open the door. I didn't want to hear one more word about Bos and Mazie. I was going to have nightmares.

Bos waved as he backed up, and I slammed the door. I twisted the deadbolt and hooked the chain. No one was going to get in.

Even though part of me felt Bos was overreacting, another part of me knew it was never a bad thing to be cautious.

I eyed the clock as I flipped my shoes off and unbuttoned my top. Kales Corners was completely stuck in the past, and my waitress uniform was a testament to that.

Sky blue, skirt to my knees, button up top, white bobby socks, and white tennis shoes. I was amazed Richard was able to see past the dreadful uniform when he looked at me, let alone actually want to date me.

I dropped my clothes as I walked to my bedroom.

Confession time. I was a horrible housekeeper.

When everyone had come over last weekend, they were lucky I had just done laundry and did a half decent clean that day. Even now, only four days later, my disaster of a duplex was growing. I was going to have to clean again before Karmen came over on Friday.

I had managed to grab a burger during work, so all I wanted to do now was take a quick shower, slip into some leggings, and fall asleep.

My phone beeped with a new text message as I stepped out of the shower, and I quickly wrapped a towel around my head.

What are you doing? Leave it to Karmen to text me all creepy after Bos scared the hell out of me.

Just got out of the shower.

Does that mean you just texted me while you were naked? And she just reached a whole new level of crazy.

No comment. I shimmied on my panties, pulled my baggy shirt over my head, and grabbed the phone to see what craziness she was up to.

I'm not sure how I feel about you texting me while your naked.

I rolled my eyes and tapped out a quick reply. **Then don't think about it. What do you want?** I pulled a brush through my hair, opting not to blow dry it because I was too damn tired for that shit, and headed to my bedroom to grab a pair of leggings.

Here was another confession.

73

I was a full-blown leggings whore.

With over seventy pairs of leggings in my closet and dresser, I could go almost four months without wearing the same pair twice. It was an addiction I was okay with. I mean, I could be addicted to drugs or something instead of leggings.

My phone echoed from the bathroom with another message from Karmen, and I grabbed the first pair of leggings my hand touched. Butter soft, covered with flowers, and to be honest, a bit gaudy. Good thing I had no plans of leaving the house in them.

I grabbed my phone from the bathroom, flipped off the light, and scrolled to her message. **I'll be there at seven Friday. Cora is coming with me.**

Awesome. I had hoped Karmen was going to bring her. **Sounds like a plan. We can go out to dinner when you get here.**

You mean breakfast.

Huh? **I thought we could go out when you got here, but if you want to wait till Saturday morning, that's fine.** I grabbed a bottle of water from the fridge and collapsed on the couch. I flipped on a rerun of some cop show and grabbed the blanket off the back of the couch.

We will be there at 7am.

What in the ever-living hell? She was going to be here that early in the morning? She was completely whacked in the head. **Uh, do you plan on watching me sleep until nine?** Karmen damn well knew I was not a morning person.

If that's what you want.

You're so weird. I texted back.

You like it.

Karmen was a nutjob. **I plead the fifth. I'm about to pass out. See you Friday.**

Can't wait.

I tossed my phone on the couch and laid back. I was exhausted. Thankfully, I only had one more day of work, and then I had off for three days. But from the sound of it, Karmen planned on taking up every single second of those three days.

My eyes closed and a light sigh echoed from my lips.

I started to mentally make a list of everything I needed to do the next day and drifted off with the TV playing in the background, and thinking of not answering the door when Karmen knocked Friday.

*

Chapter 11

Pipe

This place was a fucking hell hole.

From the outside, it looked like a well-maintained duplex, and from what I had seen from Nikki's side, hers was well kept. My side was a different fucking story.

This is what happens when you decide to rent a place sight unseen. There was a deck off the kitchen, and I knew that was where I was going to end up spending most of my time.

It had the same layout as Nikki's, but nothing was updated, the carpet was a crunchy beige, and the walls were gray, but I think they had started out white. Four of the kitchen cabinets didn't even have doors, and the kitchen faucet leaked, bad. The bathroom and bedrooms were just carbon copies of the living room and kitchen.

Thank God I planned on wooing the hell out of Nikki, and I hoped to be out of here in a month tops.

I hadn't packed much in the way of furniture, but I at least had a bed and a couch. Maniac had been cool enough to drive a cage up to Kales Corners and drop off my shit. He was making another trip today, dropping off other shit I needed. Other shit that included a coffee maker, cups, plates, and silverware. This moving out on your own shit was hard. Probably something I should have figured out in my twenties, not when I was thirty-four.

Right now, I had a bottle of water, a half pack of cigarettes, and that was it. It was at least the essentials.

Last night, I had watched Nikki come home with some old guy following her. I had to fight back the urge to go out to make sure she was okay, but I knew I couldn't come charging out of the house. She had run from me before. I didn't want to make the same mistakes; so for right now, she wasn't going to find out I was here until I wanted her to know.

Grabbing the keys to my motorcycle, my cigarettes off the counter, and headed out the door. My first mission today was to get an ally on my side.

Nikki had mentioned Alice worked at the diner in town, and I knew if I wanted to get Nikki, I was going to have to get her friends on my side. I knew Karmen liked me, although the past couple of days she had given me the eat shit look. I had to assume Nikki had told her what had happened between us. That was fixable.

I pulled up to the diner, saw four cars in the parking lot, and parked next to the door. Four bay windows lined the front of the restaurant, and I noticed everyone sitting by the window turned to watch me, Alice included. There went my idea of walking in under the radar.

"You have balls of steel," Alice hissed at me when I sat down at the counter.

I dropped my keys and cigarettes on the counter and flipped over the coffee cup in front of me. "Give me five minutes before you start laying into me, Alice. I haven't had any coffee yet."

She grabbed the coffee pot from behind her and filled my cup. "You have two minutes." She flounced off, moving around to the other tables refilling coffee cups and checking on everyone.

Two minutes were better than none.

I sipped the hot coffee and looked around the restaurant. I felt like I had been teleported back to the nineteen fifties, and at any moment, the Fonz was about to walk through the door.

Black and white tile on the floor, red and black booths, and a long counter that stretched the length of the restaurant with swiveling chairs lined in front of it.

There was a guy behind the counter, and through the window into the kitchen, he was not so secretly staring me down. This was the kind of welcome I knew I was going to get. After spending only a few hours in Kales Corners last weekend, I knew an outsider was not going to fit in easily. Especially one who rode a motorcycle and looked like me. I had left off wearing my cut today, but I knew I was still intimidating.

"What in the hell are you doing here?" Alice hissed as she sat down next to me.

"Hey, you're on the clock, Alice," the old guy in the kitchen called.

"I'm also on break, Bos. I'm entitled to those, you know."

He waved his hand at her and disappeared to the left of the window.

I sipped my coffee, and Alice watched me.

"Look here, big motorcycle man. What in the hell are you doing in Kales Corners? It better not be to see Nikki."

I looked over at her and shook my head. "I don't have a coffee maker."

"So you just thought you would drive an hour to get some of our sludge to drink? Are you insane? All that handsome wasted," she tsked.

I set down my cup and swiveled toward Alice. "I didn't just drive here for a cup of coffee. I moved here."

Alice sputtered and uncontrollably blinked her eyes about twenty times. "Come again?"

"I moved here. Specifically in the duplex next to Nikki."

She lifted her hand to my forehead and frowned. "I thought for sure you would have a fever because that is the only thing that would explain what the hell you just said."

I lifted her hand off my forehead and shook my head. "I feel fine. I'm here because I fucked up before, and this was the only way I could fix it."

"Well, you're right on the first part. You really did fuck up."

Great, Nikki had told her too what had happened. "Look, in my defense, I had no idea what the hell I was doing."

"So you did the typical male thing and decided to sleep with whatever slut tried to throw themselves at you." She crossed her arms over her chest and shook her head. "I don't know what the heck you are doing here, but I can tell you right now, Nikki is my friend, and I have no plans to go behind her back for you."

"I don't want you to go behind her back."

She crossed her arms over her chest. "So Nikki knows you are here talking to me?"

"No, I thought she could find out when she actually learns I moved here."

Alice tossed her hands in the air and stood up. "Oh, hell no. She doesn't even know you are here?"

I shook my head. "Not yet. I got into town yesterday, and she didn't get off of work until late last night."

"So why didn't you go over there this morning?"

"Because I may have only spent one night with Nikki, but I know she doesn't do anything 'til after nine in the morning."

Alice scoffed. "If that ain't the truth. She always sticks Bev and me with the early mornings. Although I don't really like working the night shift, so I'm good with that."

"I just came in here to let you know I'm here, and I have no plans of leaving unless Nikki is with me."

She crossed her arms over her chest and looked down at me. "And why the hell do you think I should believe that? You tossed her aside like she was nothing back in Weston. I really doubt you've had that big of a change of heart in a month."

"Look, I'm not going to explain this to you before I even talk to Nikki, but just know I'm not going anywhere. I don't need you on my side, but I just wanted you to know and hope you won't bash me too hard when Nikki tells you I'm here."

"I'm the friend. It's my job to bash the guy who broke my friend's heart."

I reared back. "Broke her heart?"

Alice rolled her eyes. "You really are a man," she mumbled. "Look, I'm gonna lay this out for you only in the hopes you'll leave, terrified. That night may have been fun for you, but to Nikki, that was a whole lot more than one night. She came back to you that night because she wanted to be with you but instead you had a slut in your room but you were a dumbass and were more concerned about getting your dick wet in the nearest hole. If you're only here to reenact that night and then leave, I would just leave right now. You hurt Nikki before. You do it again, and I'll cut your nuts off." She made a snipping motion with her fingers and flounced off.

Well, that was not how I expected that to go at all. My plan to possibly get Alice on my side had backfired. Now she was just more pissed off then she had been before.

I tossed a five down on the counter, grabbed my keys and cigarettes, and left the diner. I was hungry, but I was afraid Alice would spit in my food before she brought it to me.

I shoved a cigarette into my mouth, lit the end, and pulled my phone out of my pocket. "Yo," I said when Maniac answered.

"I'm about to leave. Is there anything else you need? I got all the shit you messaged me this morning."

"That should be it. You think you can stop and get some breakfast?" My stomach growled, and I glanced back at the diner. Alice was standing at the door, guarding it from me. Dammit.

"Yeah. What do you want?" Maniac asked.

"Breakfast burrito or something like that."

"Can do," Maniac mumbled. "Anything else I can pick up?"

"Nah, that should be it. I'm headed back to the house. I'll see you when you get there." I ended the call and shoved the phone in my pocket.

I swung my leg over my bike and inhaled deeply. The nicotine traveled through my body, and I relaxed a little bit.

I knew this wasn't going to be easy. Winning over Nikki's friend was going to have to happen later because right now, Nikki was my only concern.

Once Maniac got here, unloaded the rest of my shit, and had breakfast, I was going to figure out my next move.

That move was going to involve Nikki, and I couldn't help but be a little wary of how she was going to react.

I finished my cigarette, and tossed the butt on the ground, grinding it with the heel of my boot.

This wasn't going to be easy, although nothing worth it ever was.

Nikki was definitely worth it.

*

Chapter 12

Nikki

"Night, Bos."

"You sure you don't want me to follow you home?" he asked.

I shook my head and pulled my keys out of my pocket. "Nah, I'm fine. Richard would be dumb to kidnap me today. I look like hell, and I feel like crap."

"Well, get on home and get some rest. It's probably for the best you have the next three days off."

I slid into my car, and Bos waited 'til I started the car and pulled out of my parking spot before he headed around to the back of the restaurant. Work had been slow tonight, and about mid-shift, I started getting a scratchy throat and stuffy nose. I was not in the mood to get sick. Although, was anyone ever in the mood to get sick?

I navigated the short trip home and parked in front of my garage.

A bike and pickup truck were parked on the other side of the driveway, and there was a guy sitting on the porch. I couldn't see his face because it was dark, but I could see the end of his cigarette light up.

Well, this was going to be interesting. I sat in my car, trying to look like I was searching for something while I tried to catch a glimpse of my new neighbor. I'm sure he was probably seventy, smoked six packs a day, and smelled like an ashtray. I just hoped his smoke didn't blow into my open windows because I hated smoking unless it was a certain someone doing it.

I highly doubted this guy had anything on Pipe. God didn't make two men like that.

I gave up trying to catch a glimpse and decided I was either going to have to pull up my big girl panties and introduce myself to my new neighbor, or just haul my cookies in the house. "Get out of the car, Nikki," I mumbled.

Wallet in hand, and a takeout container of leftover chicken noodle soup in the other, I pushed open my door and decided I was just going to get this over with. "Evening," I called as I slammed my door.

The cigarette glowed in the dark, and I squinted trying to get a glimpse of the man. He shifted in the dark and came into the light.

Son of a gun.

Pipe Marks stood on the porch, cigarette in hand, looking like he had just stepped off the page of some motorcycle magazine.

And dammit to hell if my first thought was me wishing I was that damn cigarette.

"Evening, sugar."

*

Pipe

Well, she at least didn't look pissed off. Shocked was a better word for it.

"How was work?"

Her jaw moved up and down, but no words came out.

"Hey, I'm gonna head out, man. I gotta be up early for a run, and I don't feel like working off of a few hours of sleep." Maniac walked out the duplex and slammed the door shut behind him. He skidded to a stop when he saw Nikki standing on the other side of the driveway. "Oh hell," he muttered.

I didn't need him to see whatever the hell was going on with Nikki and me. "Sounds good, brother. I'll be rolling in around noon tomorrow, I think. Wrecker said he had some shit I need to take care of."

Maniac nodded and clapped me on the shoulder. "See ya tomorrow then." He ambled down the steps, nodded to Nikki, and backed out of the driveway.

My gaze fell back on Nikki, and I could tell she was struggling to figure out what was going on.

"What…why…what in the hell are you doing here?" she finally got out.

I looked up over my shoulder and shrugged. "As of yesterday, I live here."

The bag she had in her hand dropped to the concrete, and her jaw dropped. "You live here? As in, right next to me?"

I ran my fingers through my hair and inhaled deeply. The smoke curled around me as I exhaled, and I shrugged. "I'd have to say that was the main selling point."

"Have you lost your ever-loving mind?"

"Last I checked, no."

"Well, you better check again because if you moved here because of me, you better get back on your bike and get the hell out of here."

I shook my head. "Not yet."

Nikki snatched the bag she had dropped off of the ground. "Well, then I better be the one looking for a new place to live." She stomped to her door, fumbling with her keys in one hand, and stabbed the key into the lock. "I don't know what the hell you're up to, Pipe, but I can tell you right now, I don't want any part of it."

"You didn't say that before when I wanted a part of you."

She laughed, but it was flat and annoyed. "Oh, you definitely got a part of me last time, Pipe, and I can tell you right now, I will never make that mistake again." She shoved open the door, glared at me over her shoulder, and slammed the door shut.

"Well hell," I mumbled. I inhaled deep on my cigarette and watched her lights come on through the window. She hadn't shut the curtains before she went to work today so I could see straight into her living room.

We were going to have a talk about her closing up the house when she went somewhere. For now, though, this was working in my favor.

Nikki was working herself up into a tizzy as she slammed the white bag she had down on the counter and raked her fingers through her hair.

God damn, she was gorgeous. Even in that hideous uniform she wore, she was still sexy as fuck. Long, auburn hair flowed down her back, almost touching the curve of her ass. I remember grabbing handfuls of her hair when I slammed into her from behind, and her gasps and mewling each time I hit bottom. Fuck, she was the best I ever had.

Her fingers went to the buttons on her top, and my heart stopped. Holy fuck, she was taking off her shirt with the whole neighborhood watching. I should go pound on the window, or her doorbell to tell her to shut her curtains, but my feet were cemented to the porch.

She slipped the shirt off her shoulders and down her arms, dropping it on the floor. Her fingers went to the waistband of her skirt, and she tugged it down, kicking it off to the side.

Fuck me running. Nikki was standing in her living room in black panties that molded to the curve of her ass and a black bra. She had her back to me so I couldn't see her sweet tits, but I knew from memory what they looked like, and how soft and lush they were.

I glanced over my shoulder to make sure I was the only pervert watching. I looked back in the window, and Nikki was crouched down on the floor next to the skirt she had kicked off and pulled her phone out of one of the pockets. She put the phone to her ear and plopped down on the floor.

I shouldn't be standing there watching her, but I couldn't take my eyes off her. This was the Nikki I wanted. Uninhibited, doing whatever she wanted, and looking like a fucking angel doing it.

"Karmen," she shouted into the phone. Obviously, the soundproofing on the duplex was less than stellar. I could hear her conversation word for word.

"Did you know he was here?" she demanded. She stopped talking for two point five seconds before she went off, ranting. "Pipe fucking

Marks is living in the duplex right next to me. You're telling me you had *no* idea this was happening? I find that hard to believe since you're having his best friend's baby." She glanced out the window, but I was standing far enough off to the side to where she couldn't see me. "I call bullshit, Karmen."

Nikki stood up, moved to the window, and I took a step further into the dark losing my view of the window, but I didn't want Nikki to see me. I sat back down in the rickety chair that had been left on the porch and tossed my cigarette butt onto the driveway. It smoldered on the ground, and I pulled another one from my pack.

"I don't know why he is here. This doesn't make any sense. I walk in on the man getting his jollies with some other woman, and now bam, he's moved in right next door to me. What the hell am I supposed to do with that?"

Thankfully, I could still hear her talking. I lit the end of my cigarette and inhaled deeply as she continued to tell Karmen every reason why she thought me moving here was a bad idea.

"What the hell is he going to do here? There aren't any jobs for an MC badass."

I couldn't help but chuckle at her words. Nikki always had a funny way putting things.

"Why are you laughing? I'm dead serious." Obviously, Karmen thought Nikki was pretty funny too. "No, this isn't what I wanted, Karmen. I wanted to live far away from the man and never see him again. This is the exact God dang opposite."

I kicked my feet out and leaned back in the chair. Nikki had just confirmed the fact she had moved because of me. If that didn't make me feel like a piece of shit, I didn't know what would.

"Look, I'm going to go to sleep and wish like hell this is all a nightmare, and I'm going to wake up with Pipe living in Weston and me in Kales Corners where our paths will never cross again." Nikki's voice faded, and I knew she had moved away from the window to another part of the house where I couldn't hear her.

I sighed and ran my fingers through my hair. It was only half past nine, and I knew there was no way in hell I was going to be able to go to sleep yet.

Living in Kales Corners was going to be a huge adjustment for me, but as long as Nikki was here, I wasn't going anywhere.

*

Chapter 13

Nikki

"How does she sleep like that?"

"You would think she's suffocating herself."

"Oh my God, what if she did suffocate, and we're talking to her dead body."

"Did you really just say that? You can see her back going up and down. She's alive, dumbass."

Ugh. Waking up to Karmen and Cora fighting was not how I wanted this day to begin.

I had three pillows piled up on top of my head, and I had been sleeping like the dead 'til the Banger Sisters had shown up.

"Go away," I mumbled.

"Oh hell. She's not dead," Karmen exclaimed. "Thank God. I didn't want to have to deal with a funeral."

I grabbed pillows, pulling them off of my head. "That was the thing you were most concerned about? Not the fact your supposed best friend was dead."

Cora laughed and flopped down in the bed next to me. "How the hell do you sleep with a shit ton of pillows on your face?"

I yawned and put my arm over my eyes. "I need pitch dark to sleep."

"So, you need three pillows on your face? Don't you think one would be more than enough?"

I turned my head and glared at her. "Did you two wake me up just to ask why I had three pillows?"

"Of course not." Karmen dove onto the bed between Cora and me and burrowed under the covers. "We woke you up because we're hungry, but now that I'm laying down, I could totally go for a nap before we scavenge for food."

Cora grabbed one of my pillows and tucked it under her head. "I'm down with that. You dragging me out of bed at the ass crack of dawn sucked."

"Did you two really drive here just to take a nap?"

Karmen yawned and tucked her hands under her head. "I didn't plan on it, but I think it's the best idea ever. I wanted to make sure you were okay after your frantic call last night about Pipe." She closed her eyes and sighed deeply.

Ugh, Pipe. I had actually forgotten he was just next door. Maybe sleeping longer was a good idea. I grabbed my phone off the nightstand. "I'll set the alarm for an hour for now. If we sleep any longer than that, we'll never get out of bed."

"Make it two. It'll only be nine o'clock then."

I shook my head and reset the alarm. "I still think you're both crazy for getting here so damn early."

"Shh." Karmen patted my arm. "Sleep."

"Yeah, stop talking," Cora mumbled.

I set my phone back on the nightstand and pulled the covers up to my chin. "You're both crazy, and you better be thankful I don't yank that pillow back from you guys." I grabbed my pillow, smacked it over my head and closed my eyes.

"You love us," Karmen replied, already half asleep.

I did, even if she drove me crazy.

*

Chapter 14

Nikki

"Stop looking at me like that. The baby needs food."

Cora rolled her eyes and slipped the wrapper off her straw. "You really think he needs four eggs, sausage, bacon, a short stack of pancakes, and sourdough toast?"

Karmen took a sip of her coffee and winced. "I don't even know why I drink this anymore. Decaf blows."

I lifted my cup, inhaling the wonderful aroma of my fully caffeinated coffee and grinned. "Don't worry, I'll drink your share of coffee for you."

"Oh, you're so noble," she scoffed.

"Wooly fuck," Cora gasped.

"Wooly? What the hell?" Karmen asked.

Cora nodded her head to behind Karmen and I. "Wooly fuck."

We both turned around in the booth and saw Pipe taking a seat at the counter of the diner. "Why, that bastard," I growled.

He nodded to us but didn't come over.

"What do you think he's doing here?" Karmen asked.

I turned back around and unwrapped my fork and spoon from the napkin. "Tormenting me."

"Or ordering coffee."

I rolled my eyes at Cora and glanced over my shoulder. "Fine, ordering coffee while he torments me."

"You want me to put Ex-Lax in his coffee?" Alice topped off my coffee cup and set a carafe of syrup on the table.

"Yes," Cora and I said in unison.

"What? No, you can't do that," Karmen insisted.

We all turned to stare at her. "Whose side are you on?" Alice asked.

"The side that makes Nikki happy, and that is not the way to make her happy."

I looked up at Alice. "She's wrong. That would make me extremely happy. Do it."

"Oh shit."

I turned to look at Pipe again and saw Bos setting a cup of coffee in front of him. "That is the first time I have ever seen that man serve anyone coffee." Bos leaned against the counter and started talking to Pipe. "What in the hell?"

"You want me to go over there and put Ex-Lax in both of their coffee?"

"Does this mean no one is making my breakfast?" Karmen asked.

"That baby is making you his slave. That is exactly why I'll never have kids. I can barely take care of myself, and I like to be the one making demands, not the other way around." Cora held up her cup to Alice. "Plus, no one or no baby will ever make me stop drinking coffee."

Karmen pushed the cup away from her and crossed her arms "The kid drives me crazy sometimes, but then I think about the fact it's my and Nickel's baby, and I'll gladly give up coffee and eat like a rabid cow."

"Rabid cow? Is that what Alice was dressed up like the other weekend?"

Alice jumped, coffee sloshing over the lips of the coffee pot, and she slapped her hand over her chest. "Jesus, make a little noise the next time you're moving. How are we supposed to talk about you when you're standing right here?" She flounced off and chased Bos back into the kitchen.

"Karmen, Cora. I didn't know you guys were going to be here today."

Cora pointed her spoon at him. "Kind of like we didn't know you were going to be here. I think we're even now."

"Touché, darlin'." His eyes fell on me, and I shifted uncomfortably in the booth. "Morning, sugar."

Ugh. Damn the man for having a voice that sounded like honey dripping all over my body. "Pipe," I scowled.

"I'm heading back to Weston for a bit. You ladies need anything?"

Cora set her spoon down. "A Starbucks."

Pipe laughed, the sound rich and deep. "Not sure I can fit that on the back of my bike."

Cora shrugged her shoulder. "It was worth a try. I'll have to deal with this sludge for the weekend."

"Weekend?" Pipe asked.

"Cora and I are staying with Nikki until Sunday," Karmen explained.

"I see. Well, you guys have a good weekend. I'm sure I'll see you around." Pipe tipped his head and thankfully left the diner.

Cora fanned herself with her hand and pointed at me. "I'm not at all into that man, but can I just say you must have nerves of steel to ignore him the way you just did. I swear, if any guy would look at me the way he does you, my panties would burst into flames on the spot."

"You're not helping," Karmen hissed.

Cora put her hand down and leaned forward. "I thought you said we were here to help her figure out what the hell she wanted. I say what she wants is another roll in the hay with that man."

Karmen tossed her hands in the air. "You think you could be a little bit more subtle?"

Cora shook her head. "Subtly is not in my vocabulary. You want him, take him, Nikki."

I cleared my throat and played with my fork and spoon. "I tried that. He was with another chick."

Cora rolled her eyes. "Can I lay something out for you and you not get mad?"

I looked over at Karmen who shrugged her shoulders. 'Sure, I guess."

"That man that just walked out that door is your typical biker. Thinks he knows exactly what he wants but honestly doesn't know a damn thing. Karmen gave me a brief rundown of what happened between you two, and I'm not surprised at all."

"You're not surprised about what?" I asked.

"I'm not surprised you two knocked boots, probably damn good by my indication, and he ran for the hills into the arms of the nearest whore because you scared the living hell out of him. He's lived in a world where he calls the shots, and you're making him feel something he doesn't know how to deal with."

"I get what you're saying, but then why the hell did he move here?"

Cora sat back in the booth and smiled. "Because Pipe came to his senses. A lot quicker than I've ever seen before actually. My mom and dad did the dance you two are doing, except it took them almost ten years to get on the same page."

"Your parents went through this for ten years? It's only been two months since Pipe and I hooked up, and I'm ready to run away and become a nun."

Cora shook her head. "You do that, and you're stupid. Pipe wants you, Nikki. It's plain as day."

I rolled my eyes. "Yeah, he wants to have sex with me again, that's about it."

"See, now this is where the ball is firmly in your court, and you get to be the one to call the shots."

Karmen clapped her hands together and did a little shimmy in the booth. "I knew it. I thought he just ran because he was a dumbass, and I was right. This is so awesome." Karmen high-fived Cora and looped her arm around my shoulders. "Now, how to make him grovel."

I shrugged off her arm and shook my head. "No. You guys are wrong. I know these guys in the MC think they can do whatever they want, but they can't. Not in the real world."

Cora rolled her eyes. "They are in the real world, Nikki. Every guy thinks the same way they do. These bikers just take every liberty they can and run with it. I've lived in an MC all of my life, and trust me when I say I know what I'm talking about. Pipe is done doing the typical male shit. No man moves an hour away from his club for just a piece of pussy."

I blinked slowly, taking in her words. "I need more coffee." I had resigned myself to the idea that Pipe didn't want me, and now here he was living next to me, and Cora was telling me that was a huge step.

A grin spread across Cora's lips, and she crossed her arms over her chest. "You get it, but you don't want to admit it. Just make that man grovel, Nikki, and you'll get it soon enough."

"What'd I miss?" Alice set down Karmen's huge platter of food in front of her and put her hands on her hips. "You look like you've seen a ghost," she said looking down at me.

Karmen patted my shoulder and reached for the syrup. "She'll be fine eventually. Cora just laid a load of information on her that she's struggling to process."

"Well, was it good information?"

Cora kicked me under the table, and I jumped a bit. "In time it will be."

I sighed and watched Alice bustle back to the kitchen to get the rest of our breakfast.

That was good information?

More like it was information so confusing I had no idea what was what anymore, and all I wanted to do was crawl back into my bed and never surface.

"Chin up, buttercup," Karmen smirked. "You have a badass motorcycle man who wants back in your bed. Make him work for it."

Jesus. That was easier said than done.

Life was so much easier when I thought Pipe didn't want me anymore.

*

Chapter 15

Pipe

"Holy fuck. I didn't expect to see you for a week."

I sat down to the right of Wrecker and tossed my phone on the long table. "Yeah, well, the red carpet wasn't exactly rolled out for me when I hit Kales Corners." That was a damn understatement. The two interactions I had with Nikki were less than promising.

"So what? You gave up?"

"Nah, just regrouping. Karmen and Cora came to visit her all weekend, so I don't really think I'm going to get any of her time."

"Nice excuse."

"You back already? I thought for sure Nikki was going to put up more of a fight than that." Nickel walked into church and took the seat on Wrecker's left.

I scoffed and shook my head. "Nah, she's still there. With your ol' lady, by the way. Thank you for that. Now I really can't get to her."

Nickel grinned. "You really think I had any say over that? Right now, I'm at Karmen's mercy until she pushes out that baby. One wrong word and she turns on the waterworks. I avoid that shit like the plague, brother. You don't want her there? You tell her."

Yeah, that wasn't going to happen. "She'll be gone Sunday. I can wait until then."

"Wise man," Nickel mumbled.

Brinks, Maniac, Clash, and Slayer filed into the room and took their places around the table.

"Where the hell is Boink?" Wrecker asked.

Nickel cleared his throat. "Last I saw, he was stumbling to his bed at six this morning when Karmen and Cora left."

"Jesus Christ. It's like herding cats with you fuckers. When he manages to fall out of bed, make sure you tell him he's cleaning the whole common room for missing church," Wrecker growled.

"Well, just look at it this way," Clash chuckled. "You'll never need to have kids with the seven of us around."

"Yeah, seven dumbass sons." Wrecker grabbed the gavel in front of him and crashed it down on the table. "Let's get this shit over with. Cora."

"Uh, what about her?" Slayer asked.

"Where the hell is she?"

Nickel looked around. "Um, she's up in Kales Corners with Karmen, like Pipe said. I figured with Pipe living next door, it was fine for her to go."

"What part of she needs to have someone on her at all times was hard for you to understand. You think your woman and Nikki are going to keep her safe?" Wrecker barked.

"How much trouble can those three get into, really?" Brinks asked.

Nickel leaned forward and looked down the table at him. "Have you met Karmen? She's a crazy wildcard at the moment."

"Then why the hell did you send her to Kales Corners with Cora?"

Nickel stood up and pointed at me. "I damn well told you. Pipe was there to watch them."

"Don't you think maybe you should have run that shit by me?" I drawled. If I had known I was supposed to hang around, I would have.

"I didn't think you would run with your tail between your legs not even forty-eight hours later. I thought you had balls of steel, man. I figured you would throw her over your shoulder, tell her what the hell was going to happen, and that would be it." Nickel fell back into his chair, disgusted.

I pulled a cigarette from my pocket and stuck it in the corner of my mouth.

Wrecker turned to me and shook his head. "No smoking in here, dumbass."

"Since fucking when?"

"Since I said so."

I ripped the cigarette out of my mouth and tossed it on the table next to my phone.

"Can I ask a question?" Slayer said.

"This oughta be good," Clash chuckled.

Slayer smacked him on the back of the head. "Shut it, dick."

Clash flipped him off and scooted his chair closer to Nickel. "Abusive asshole," he muttered under his breath.

"Fucking cats," Wrecker mumbled under his breath. "What the fuck is your question?" he growled at Clash.

He cleared his throat and looked around the table. "I might have missed this, but do we know why we need to keep an eye on Cora? I mean, she's just Jenkins' sister. What could possibly be going on with her?"

Wrecker leaned back in his chair. "It's not what she did, it's what Jenkins is getting his club into. I know you all are starting to hate all of these runs we are doing, realizing we are getting into deep shit when what you don't realize is that Jenkins is fucking knee deep in the shit."

"You've told us all of this before," Maniac drawled. "I, for one, would like to know exactly what the fuck you are talking about you when you say, 'knee deep in shit.'" He leaned forward and clasped his hands in front of him.

"Yeah, I don't think that's too much to ask for. We are putting ourselves on the line for some chick we don't even know, and furthermore, for a club and president that no one at this table can stand," Nickel agreed.

Wrecker stroked his beard and eyed everyone at the table. "The problem with you guys knowing more about what is going on is I don't even know anything more than what I just told you."

"Then why the hell don't we demand to know more. You think Jenkins or anyone in River Valley would put their ass on the line for us? I fucking doubt it." Maniac slammed his hand down on the table, and Clash, Slayer, and Brinks all grunted their agreeance.

"Look, I get where you guys are coming from, but I think busting into River Valley with our dicks swinging demanding answers isn't the way we need to go about this."

"I agree with Wrecker." I shifted in my chair and pointed to Nickel. "You've been restless for a while. I get that, and you and I talked about the effects of you jumping ship and rushing into opening a new chapter. You think you all have it bad now, you don't know the shit Jenkins would bring down on a new club. Here in Weston, we are established, popping up wanting a new chapter opens the door for you to be Jenkins' whipping boy."

Nickel shook his head. "I don't want a new chapter anymore, I just want Jenkins to get out of the business of Weston. You don't see us poking around in the bullshit he's gotten himself into, do you? Instead, he's pouring that bullshit over each chapter, fucking everyone over."

Wrecker stood up and leaned over the table, his hands braced in front of him. "Listen up, and listen real good. I hear everything you guys are saying, and I agree with it all. I want more than anything to go back to the club we were when all we had to worry about was who was buying the keg for the party. Unfortunately, those days are fucking gone. I'm not saying we will never have them back, I'm just saying to get them back, we need to tread very carefully. Because if we pull out, we not only upset Jenkins, we upset everyone he has tangled himself with."

Brinks smashed his finger into the table. "But we didn't make those fucking deals, Jenkins did."

A smirk spread across Wrecker's lips. "So you think they'll care about that? We can just skip on over to them, tell them we are out and if they have a problem with it they can just deal with Jenkins, right? Come on, Brinks, you're supposed to be the smart one of the group."

"Find out who the deal is made with, and I bet we can find a way to get out of them without any bloodshed," Brinks insisted.

Wrecker turned to me. "Brinks lives in a fucking fairytale land with unicorns and rainbows."

A chuckle escaped my lips, and Brinks growled. "I know what the fuck I'm talking about."

Wrecker threw his hands up in the air. "Fine, rainbow, you win. I'll get whatever information you need, and you can ride off on your unicorn and save us all. Sound like a plan to all you fucking idiots?" Wrecker stormed out of church, slamming the door shut behind him.

"Does that mean Brinks' name is now Rainbow?" Maniac asked.

"No, you fucking idiot, it means you all need to chill the fuck out. Wrecker and I don't like this muling bullshit any more than you all do, but for now, it's what we do." I stood up and grabbed my phone, stuck my discarded cigarette in my mouth, and looked at the guys. "Try not to piss off Wrecker too much while I'm gone. With Cora up in Kales Corners with Nikki and Karmen, I won't be back until Monday."

"I can go up there if you need me to," Nickel volunteered.

I shook my head. "You don't need to. Now if you wanna go up to see your woman, knock yourself out. But I'll take care of Cora."

The guys relaxed back in their chairs and started talking about what they were going to do this weekend. I shoved my phone in my pocket and set out to find Wrecker. As much as I didn't want to have to deal with him when he was pissed off, I needed to talk before I left for the three days.

I walked into the common room and saw him behind the bar downing shots. "It's only eleven o'clock. Starting pretty early, huh?"

Wrecker glared at me and refilled his glass. "Dealing you fucking idiots would make a saint drink."

"What about a unicorn?" I laughed.

He shook his head and tossed back the shot. "Fucking Brinks. Always sitting back, watching, and smart as a damn whip. Then he suggests we just nicely ask to be released from whatever shit we're in like we're letting them know we can't make it to the damn dance next week."

I ran my fingers through my hair and tried not to laugh. "Rainbows, unicorns, and now dances. You sure the president of an MC?"

Wrecker growled. "I don't fucking know since half of those pansies in there are chicken shits."

I shrugged and leaned against the bar. "They have a point, Wrecker. We're putting our asses on the line for something that isn't benefiting us at all. We don't see any of the money Jenkins gets off these runs."

Wrecker slammed his glass down on the bar. "I fucking know it, Pipe. I tried to fight it at the beginning, and I couldn't. Jenkins has some powerful friends that were more than ready to come to Weston and make us bend any which way they felt right. Agreeing was better than taking a stand and all of us getting our faces rearranged."

I held up my hands. "Look, I get that too. I'm fucking Switzerland in this. I get the guys, and I get you. Now we have to figure out a way to get what everyone wants."

Wrecker hung his head. "I don't fucking sleep at night because all I do is lay awake trying to find some exit strategy to get out of this, but there isn't one, Pipe. We're fucking stuck."

I sighed and lit the end of my cigarette. "Don't tell me to put it out," I threatened. Wrecker rolled his eyes but kept his mouth shut. "What if you try what Brinks said?"

"Pipe, don't tell me I'm going to have fucking call you Periwinkle now. I told you that shi—"

I held up my hand and shook my head. "I'm not saying we simply ask to be out. I'm saying we do what Brinks said, find out who is at the core of this. Try to work a way that maybe we get in their good graces and work this situation in our favor. You and I both know we *aren't* getting anything from this right now, so I say we find a way *to* benefit from this shit."

Wrecker sighed and grabbed the bottle from me. "Fine. I want you to head back to Kales Corners and keep an eye on Cora. I'll try to work with the guys without calling them fucking idiots."

I leveled my gaze on Wrecker and busted out laughing. "We both know that's bullshit." Wrecker was known for calling anyone and everyone a fucking idiot at one point or another.

"Yeah, yeah. Get the fuck out of here and keep an eye on the girls." Wrecker filled his glass and tossed back another shot. "Call me Monday, and I'll let you know if we need you back here. I know you got shit going on with your woman, so I'll try to rely more on Nickel 'til you get your shit straight."

"Thanks, brother, but you know I'm here whenever you need me."

He waved me off and lumbered back toward church where all of the guys were still waiting.

I inhaled deep on my cigarette and closed my eyes. The nicotine coursed through me, and I sighed deeply. This was shit, but we at least had a plan now.

Were we going to make any headway? Who the hell knew?

I had planned to spend the day in Weston, but now that someone had to be on Cora, and I was volunteered for that duty for the next three days, I needed to get back to Kales Corners.

The one good thing about keeping an eye on Cora was I was going to be close to Nikki, whether she liked it or not.

*

Chapter 16

Nikki

"Oh, I brought a game!"

Cora rolled her eyes and kicked her feet up on the couch. "Are we in first grade?"

Karmen ignored her and raced to the bedroom.

"I'm gonna order a pizza, but someone has to go pick it up." I grabbed my phone and scrolled to the number for The Shack.

"They don't even have pizza delivery in this town. How in the hell do you live here?" Cora complained.

"The pizza place is two blocks away. I can walk to get it." I put the phone to my ear and waited for Pete or John to answer the phone. Yes, I was on first name basis with the pizza place.

Karmen came bounding out of the bedroom when Pete answered the phone. "Nikki," he called. "The usual?"

Lordy. I had only been in town over a month, and I already had a usual order at the pizza place. "Um, yes, but double it." If I could polish off a small extra cheese pizza by myself, I knew I was going to need more to feed us. "Actually, triple it." It had been a few hours since the last time Karmen ate, and I knew she had to be close to starving.

"Ready in twenty minutes."

I hung the phone up, checking the time. "I gotta leave in fifteen minutes. Who's going to walk with me?"

"Not it," Karmen and Cora called at the same time.

I rolled my eyes and set my phone on the counter. "You're both fair weather bitches. I'll go get the pizza by myself."

"It's only five minutes away," Cora snickered. "Just take your car, and it'll only take you two."

Karmen held up a box and did a little shuffle. "Stop talking and look at me," she hollered.

"What in the devil is that?" Cora squinted at the box and leaned forward. "Is that a box full of dicks?"

"Yup, sure is," Karmen sang out as she lowered the box and took the cover off.

"You know, it's always the pregnant ones that are freaks. Coming out here with a box of dicks," Cora mumbled. She sat back on the couch and watched Karmen sit on the floor and pull some cards out of the box.

"It's like the memory game where you have a bunch of cards in front of you, and you flip over two at a time trying to match them," she explained.

"Um, yeah. But isn't that with like fruit or something?" I asked.

"Yes, if you're playing the kid version. This is the adult version." She tossed the cover at me, and I caught it midair.

"Dick Match," I read out loud. "Jesus, they will make a game out of anything, won't they?"

Karmen tossed me a few cards, and I busted out laughing.

"What?" Cora demanded. "What the hell is so funny about a bunch of cards with dicks on them?"

I tossed her a card and watched her cheeks flush. "The fact they hilariously named them. Nothing like holding the Sergeant Penis in your hand, huh?"

Cora tossed it back at Karmen and slid off the couch to check out the rest of the cards. "This is hilariously gross," she mumbled, inspecting another card. "Why do you think this one is called Steve?"

"Oh wait," Karmen replied. "This one is Steve's friend."

"Yup, this isn't strange at all, you guys." I shook my head and headed into the kitchen. "I think this game calls for wine and snacks." I grabbed one of the four bottles of wine we had bought at the store today and the extra-large tub of licorice Karmen had insisted we needed.

"Don't forget my wine," Karmen called.

I grabbed her bottle of non-alcoholic cranberry grape wine and three glasses. "I just don't know why you didn't buy grape juice?" I asked as I dropped down on the carpet next to them.

"Because this is fizzy, and juice isn't. It mimics wine in a half-assed way."

A knock sounded at the door, and we all looked at each other. "I thought you said they don't deliver?"

"They don't," I mumbled as I stood up. "Did you call Nickel and tell him to come up here?"

"What? Hell no. This is a girls' weekend. I told him I would see him Sunday afternoon," Karmen insisted.

"Then who the hell is at the door," I mumbled as I twisted the lock and unhooked the chain. I wasn't afraid of Richard anymore, but I decided it never hurt to be safe.

I opened the door a crack and peeped out.

"Sugar."

Oh hell. I really shouldn't be surprised he was knocking on my door, but I was. I had figured that he was still in Weston, and had hoped he would stay there all weekend.

"Go away."

A smirk spread across the hot idiot's lips, and my icy demeanor melted a smidge. "I can't. I'm here on club business."

"What in the hell do I have to do with club business?" I swung the door wide open and propped my hand on my hip.

"Not you, her." He nodded over my shoulder, and I looked at Karmen and Cora who were sprawled out on the floor with fifty dick cards surrounding them.

"Her who?" I asked. "Is something wrong with Nickel?"

"Nickel?" Karmen chirped. "I just texted him five minutes ago. Nothing is wrong with him."

"Cora."

"Oh man, what the hell now? Don't tell me that overbearing bearded behemoth says I need to come back to that shit hole club," Cora whined.

Pipe shook his head. "You don't need to come back, but I do need to keep an eye on you while you're here."

I rolled my eyes and tried shutting the door. Pipe's foot shot out and blocked the door. "You can keep an eye on her from your side of the duplex. We have no plans of leaving tonight," I informed him.

"Well, Cora and I don't plan on leaving. Nikki needs to go pick up our pizza."

"Pizza?" Pipe tilted his head to the side. "I haven't had dinner yet."

"Oh really? Then I guess you better go fire up the microwave and eat whatever TV dinner you had planned for tonight." I kicked at his foot, hoping to throw him off balance, but the man was like a damn rock.

"Still sassy as ever," he mumbled low.

"Why don't we make Pipe go get the food?" Karmen suggested.

"Because I'm supposed to be keeping an eye on Cora, not your pizza."

"Details, details," Cora muttered. "How about you go get your pizza, and then you can hang out with us tonight."

"What?" I squawked. "He is not hanging out with us."

"Then you have to change out of those bright ass leggings and haul your cookies to the pizza place in about thirty seconds," Karmen laughed.

"What's wrong with my leggings? Leggings are pants." I looked down at my legs and stepped back from the door.

Pipe pushed open the door and slammed it shut behind him. "You look hot, but you can't wear those out of the house."

"And why the hell not?"

"Because you may technically be covered from head to toe, but with those pants or whatever you called them, I can see every inch of your long, toned legs." He leaned close and whispered in my ear. "I like 'em though, sugar."

"Whoa Lord. I felt that all the way over here." Cora fanned herself with her hand. "My dry spell is catching up to me."

Karmen cackled and looked down at the cards in front of them. "I'm sure looking at all of these dicks isn't helping." She held up a card. "I'm sure the Steve is all kinds of turning you on right now."

Cora wrinkled her nose. "Lord help me, I hope I never meet another Steve in my life because all I'm going to picture is that card."

"Can we focus for like two seconds? I'm not changing my pants, and since all three of you say I can't leave the house in my leggings, then who is going to get the pizza?"

"Not it," Cora and Karmen said in unison again. They were getting damn good at that.

"Jesus. Fine. I'll go get the pizza, but I'm going to need your phone number." Pipe looked down at me.

"What? Mine? Why me? You're keeping an eye on Cora, not me."

"I don't have a cell phone," Cora replied.

I'm pretty sure my eyes bugged out of my head, and my jaw dropped. "You don't have a phone? How do you keep in contact with, well, anyone?" Was that even possible in this day and age?

"No phone, so you're going to have to give him your number." Cora shrugged her shoulders. "Sorry, chica."

Pipe pulled out his phone and looked at me expectantly. I rambled off the number, and he punched it into his phone. "Where's the pizza place?" he asked as he shoved his phone back in his pocket. "And, I need a car."

"What, why? You can walk," I insisted.

Karmen stood up, pulled her keys out of her pocket, and handed them to Pipe. "You can take mine." Karmen looked at me and smiled. "It may only be two blocks away, but I wouldn't want to walk that with a pile of pizzas in my arms either."

She had a point, but Pipe was strong enough to walk with a few boxes in his arms. "Whatever," I scoffed."

"You need me to get anything else while I'm out?" He eyed the full bottle of wine on the floor. "I see you guys already started the party, so I'm your only chance to get something you forgot."

I waved my hand at him and sat down next to Karmen. "We're good. All we need is pizza."

Pipe nodded and pocketed Karmen's keys. "Try not to get into any trouble while I'm gone."

"We managed all day without you," Cora called. "I'm sure we'll survive another ten minutes."

Pipe shook his head and slipped out the door.

Karmen slugged me in the shoulder. "Good God, woman. You sure do know how to flip your bitch switch. I get you want the man to grovel, but you keep up the charade you want him gone, he might actually disappear."

Cora grabbed the bottle of wine and the corkscrew. "She's right. I know I told you to make the man grovel, but you have to remember, he's a biker who thinks he calls the shots."

I shook my head. "You were the one who said it was my turn to call the shots."

Cora pulled the cork out and grabbed a glass. "I did say that, and you need to, but you need to do it in a way he thinks he is still calling the shots." Cora filled a glass and handed it to me. "You're gonna have to be smart about this, girl. You want that man no matter what bullshit you spew about hating him."

I took a sip of my wine and swirled it around in the glass. "Okay, I don't hate him, but come on, Cora, I caught him with another chick."

She filled her glass and grabbed Karmen's bottle of fake wine. "Lord, I gotta lay another truth on you." She filled a glass for Karmen and handed it to her.

"Oh Lord, I think I know what you're about to say, and now I feel like I need a real drink." Karmen downed the glass in three swallows and held it to Cora for a refill. "Lay it on us."

Cora rolled her eyes and filled Karmen's glass again. "I feel like a damn bartender," she muttered as she set the bottle down. "So, you weren't dating him, Nikki. You guys were nothing. Sure, to you it was more, and it was more to Pipe, but he was too much of an idiot to see that. You had one night together, and a fuck of a lot of sexual tension, but you weren't attached to him in any way."

I ducked my head. "I know. Well, at least my head knows that. My heart hates him, and my body wants him."

Karmen wrapped her arm around my shoulder and pulled me to her side. "So, we just need to get your head, heart, and body on the same page. Easy peasy."

I leaned my head on her shoulder. "I'm such an idiot. Why did I have to sleep with Pipe? If I had just ignored the damn man, none of this would have happened."

"You don't ignore a man like that," Cora pointed out.

"You did."

She shook her head. "I'm immune to all of these assholes because of my brother. I will never ever screw or date a guy who is part of an MC."

"Hey, Nickel is pretty fantastic," Karmen added.

"I'm not saying he isn't. I'm just saying I don't want a guy in an MC. Pipe is a pretty cool guy too, but again, just not the type of guy I want."

"Maybe I'm the same. I'm not destined to be with a guy who is in an MC."

Cora shook her head. "If that were the case, you never would have fallen into bed with him."

I took a sip and looked to the side. "I didn't fall into bed with him."

"Oh really?" Karmen scoffed. "Just what exactly would you call it then?"

"Um, it was more like a push…up against the wall." My cheeks heated, and I knew they were a lovely shade of pink.

"You dirty whore," Cora cackled. "It's always the quiet ones."

"Pfft, Nikki is hardly a quiet one." Karmen rolled her eyes and pushed me away.

"Hey," I objected. "I'm not sure if I should be offended by that or not."

Another knock sounded at the door. "Open up. This shit is hot," Pipe called.

"Wow, that was quick." Karmen popped up from the floor and opened the door.

"Jesus, you see how fast she got up when there was food at stake?" Cora laughed.

Karmen flipped us off and moved back to let Pipe in the door. "Y'all don't even know what you're talking about. I'm not kidding when I say this kid has complete control over me."

"That'll last for at least eighteen years," Pipe mumbled. He dropped the pizza on the counter. "Holy fuck, that shit is molten. What the hell did you order?"

"Three cheese pizzas with extra cheese, and breadsticks." I opened the box on top, and my stomach growled. "Lots of breadsticks with extra garlic."

Pipe waved his hand in front of his face. "We won't have to worry about vampires for the next ten years," he mumbled.

"Oh my God, that smells heavenly." Karmen slammed the door and floated over to the pizza. "I need a plate in my hand, or I'm going to just take a whole box for myself."

"Well, that was the plan until you guys invited Pipe over, so now we need plates."

Karmen grabbed a box from the bottom, flipped it open, grabbed four breadsticks, throwing them on top of the pizza, and sat down. "You mean you guys are going to need plates. I don't."

"Oh hell," Cora mumbled. "I like the way you think." Cora shot up from the floor, grabbed a box just like Karmen did, and tossed some breadsticks on top. "Looks like you two are going to have to share." She tossed a wink at me over her shoulder and plopped down on the couch next to Karmen.

And that is when I realized my friends were traitors.

"Oh, my God, my brain is screaming feed me, and my body is like hell yes." Karmen lifted a breadstick to her lips and winked. "Thank God they are on the same page."

Such a bitch. "I need to find new friends."

Pipe smiled at me, and I had to fight my body from moving into him. "I'll get a plate, and you can have the box. Or vice versa. Whatever works for you, sugar."

What worked for me was Pipe grabbing a few slices of pizza and heading back to his place to eat them. "I'll get a plate. I'm not that hungry." I had been starving half an hour ago, but now my appetite had vanished, and my stomach was in knots.

Everything Cora had said about Pipe rattled around in my head as I grabbed a plate and then nabbed two pieces of pizza.

"You sure that's all you want?" he asked as he eyed my plate. "From the smell coming off this pizza, I know as soon as I get a bite in my mouth, I'm not going to be able to stop."

I gulped and nodded. "I'm good." I was far from being good, but Pipe didn't need to know I was thinking about all the things I'd like him to do with his mouth and never stop.

"What the hell kind of game were you guys playing?" Pipe kicked at the cards on the floor and stretched out next to them. He set down the box of pizza and picked up one of the cards. "What the fuck?" he flipped it around and held it up. "What the fuck is a Steve penis?"

Karmen busted out laughing, and I couldn't help but smile. "That's Cora's next boyfriend." I sat down in the recliner and balanced my plate in my lap. "Although, I think she liked the Duke of Wellington."

Cora snickered. "Would that make me a duchess then?"

Karmen choked on her pizza, and Cora even got a chuckle out of Pipe.

Pipe tossed the card on the floor and shook his head. "So this is what a girls' night looks like, huh? I'll have to let the boys know there aren't naked pillow fights."

"You missed that already," Karmen smirked. "Cora got mad that I hit her in the face, so she tit-punched me. Tit punches ruin everything."

Now it was Pipe's turn to choke on his pizza. "Holy fuck, woman," he wheezed. He pounded on his chest, and I took mercy on him by handing him the bottle of wine.

He took a swig and sputtered. "What the fuck is this, juice?"

"Oh, whoops. That's Karmen's bottle."

He looked at the label and shook his head. "Fucking sparkling juice. It's like I'm at the kiddie table at Thanksgiving."

"Hey, don't knock it. Hand it over, jerk. That's all I can have until I push this little badass out."

Pipe handed her the bottle and settled back on the carpet. "You find out it's a boy?"

"Huh, no, why?"

He shoved his mouth full of pizza and waved his hand. "You just called it a little badass."

"Um, yeah. That doesn't mean it's a boy, though. Girls can be little badasses too," Karmen pointed out.

"Yeah, look at me, being all badass and shit," Cora laughed.

Pipe shook his head. "Yeah, you look like a badass in your fuzzy slippers."

"Badasses get cold feet too." She tucked her feet under her and balanced her pizza box in her lap. "Now, why don't we put on a movie so my badassness can stop being put into question." Cora flipped off Pipe and nodded at me. "Stick one in, chica. Once this one next to me gets her belly full, you know she's going to pass out for a couple of hours."

"Hey," Karmen protested, "I want you to grow a little badass in your belly and not get tired."

"Not happening," Cora whispered.

"I think you're the only one in this room that wants a little badass in their belly at the moment," I chuckled. I dropped my plate onto the recliner and crouched down in front of the cabinet. My eyes connected with Pipe's, and I couldn't rip my gaze away from him.

He looked uncertain and surprised at what I had said. He lowered his eyes to his plate, and I quickly looked for a movie and plopped back down in my chair after sticking it in.

"What'd you pick?" Cora asked.

"The new Transformer movie," I mumbled as the previews started playing.

"Hell yes, I can totally get down with some Mark Wahlberg blowing stuff up." Cora rubbed her hands together and nodded to the bottle of wine next to my chair. "Make yourself useful, Pipe, and fill our glasses. You invaded our girls' night, so now you have to be our waiter."

He shook his head but reached over and grabbed the bottle. "Not by choice, darlin'." He topped off our glasses and moved to the fridge where he grabbed two bottles of beer.

If only the guys from the club could see him now.

"You need any more pizza, sugar?" He looked at me, my glass of wine in his hand.

"Uh, no. I'll be fine with this." I grabbed the glass from his hand and set it on the small table next to my chair. "Thank you," I whispered.

"Anything else I can get for you?"

I gulped and got a glance of Cora and Karmen on the couch leaning toward us trying to hear what Pipe was saying. Damn heifers. "I could use a blanket, but I'll get it."

"Tell me where it is."

"Right here," Cora called right before my deep teal blanket hit him in the back of his head. He reached behind him, snatching it before it hit the ground, and opened it up. He looked expectantly at me, and I realized he was waiting for me to move my plate so he could spread the blanket over me.

"Okay," I whispered as I lifted my plate. He draped the blanket over my lap and looked down at me again. "Erg, thank you." Gah, what in the hell was going on? This big, tough-looking man was looking like he wanted to pull back the blanket and sit down with me in the chair.

"Anything you want, sugar." Karmen and Cora both sighed loudly, and it took everything I had to not tell them to put a sock in it.

Pipe finally moved, laying down in front of my chair, and Cora tossed a pillow at his head. "Here," she called. "Don't say I never did anything for you."

He grabbed the pillow, tucked it under his head, and pulled the box of half-eaten pizza to him.

We watched the movie with Karmen passing out ten minutes in, and Cora knocking out halfway through.

Pipe laid on the hard floor, the pillow tucked under his head, and I had to sit on my hands so I didn't get up and lie down next to him.

Cora had been right when she said Pipe and I weren't together when he had slept with that other chick. It had hurt seeing, but I couldn't rightfully be mad at him for it. I watched Pipe more than I watched the movie. I had written him off, and now he was back in my life, and I had to figure out what I wanted to do.

Pipe looked pretty good lying on my floor. Now I had to decide if I wanted him back in my bed and life permanently.

*

Chapter 17

Pipe

"Wake up."

I tossed my arm over face and rolled over.

"Pipe, wake up. You're gonna be sore in the morning if you sleep on the floor all night."

"Slept in worse places, sugar," I mumbled.

"Well, I don't care. Get off my floor."

I moved my arm and opened my eyes to see Nikki standing over me. "Sugar."

"Don't sugar me. I just wrestled Karmen and Cora into bed. I'm not really in the mood to do it with you." She rubbed her arm. "Damn, Karmen has a hell of a right hook if you wake her up."

"You okay?"

"I'll be better when I can finally go to sleep. Between the three of you conking out by the middle of the movie and taking turns sawing logs, there was no way I was going to fall asleep." She grabbed the remote off of the side table and turned off the TV. "Now, get up."

"What time is it?" I half sat up, leaning back on my elbows.

"Ten-thirty."

Shit. There was no way in hell I was going to be able to go back to sleep now. I was lucky to get three hours of uninterrupted sleep a night. My little *siesta* at nine-thirty wasn't going to bode well for me sleeping anymore. "I'll get out of your hair, sugar." If she was tired, she didn't need me bugging her.

"You're fine. I just didn't think the floor could be very comfortable."

I stood up and brushed my hand down my shirt. "Like I said, I've slept in far worse places."

She rolled her eyes. "I'm not in the mood to hear stories of your debauchery."

I shook my head. "Not what I'm talking about. Once I hit eighteen, I never slept in a shit place, because I always had a home with the Lords."

She tilted her head, and her hair fell in her eyes. "What about before you turned eighteen?"

I reached out, not even thinking, and brushed her hair back. She froze instantly, and I knew I had crossed a line. I took a step back and put my hands in my pockets. "I was in and out of foster homes."

"What?"

"Um, I said I was in foster care. My parents didn't want me when I was born. I lived in a shit county that didn't try to find me adoptive parents, so I lived in about ten foster homes before I aged out of the system."

"I'm sorry."

"Not a big deal. Lots of kids go through it, I was just lucky to make it out."

"Um, I was in foster care too," she whispered. "My dad died when I was six, and my mom couldn't handle it."

"Fuck, sugar." I didn't care if I had a shit life, but I didn't want that for Nikki.

She shrugged and ran her fingers through her hair. "It was like my mom wanted me, but she missed my dad real bad, and then got into drugs."

Her voice was quiet and timid. "Nikki, you don't have to tell me. It's okay."

She ignored me completely. "I remember coming home from school, and my mom was passed out at the kitchen table. She was still breathing, but I couldn't wake her up. I ran upstairs pounding on all of the neighbor's doors until someone answered. We didn't live in a nice apartment, but thankfully the person who answered my frantic knocking helped me. Social Services scooped me up so quickly, I didn't even see if my mom was okay. They kept telling me over and over she was fine, but I couldn't live with her anymore. I got it, but there was still a side that just wanted my mom." She shook her head and looked down at the floor. "I have no idea why I just told you that."

"I don't either, sugar, but I'll listen. Whatever you want to say, I'm here."

She looked up with tears in her eyes. "But for how long?"

"How long for what?"

She swiped at her nose and looked to the right. "How long are you here for, Pipe?"

I didn't know what to say. What was the right thing to say? For as long as she wanted me here? "I…well…"

She put her hand on my face and shook her head. "Nevermind. Get out." She stalked to the door and threw it open.

Fuck.

"Nikki, look, I don't know—"

"I know you don't know, Pipe. That's the damn problem."

I grabbed her hand and pulled her to me. She tried to pull away, but I wasn't going to let her go before I said what I need to. "I don't know what to say to make this shit better."

"Well, you need to say something. Something more than you don't know."

"I'm sorry."

She threw her head back and laughed. "You're sorry for what? For being a man? For sleeping with me? You're sorry for even meeting me? What the hell are you sorry for, because from where I'm standing, there's a list of things."

"I'm sorry about that night. I didn't know." Mother fuck, this shit was hard. Who the hell wanted to sit around and talk about their feelings?

"You didn't know what?"

Fuck. This was like pulling teeth. My fucking teeth. "I didn't know what the fuck to do with you. We had fucking amazing sex and then I had no idea what to do. I've never been with a chick and actually wanted to be around her when we weren't having sex."

"So what? I was just supposed to hang around until you pulled your head out of your ass and decided you actually wanted to talk to me when my clothes were on?" She crossed her arms over her chest and glared at me.

I was losing ground fast. "I did spend time with you before we had sex when your clothes were on. It was after we had sex I couldn't figure out how to still have sex with you and you know, hang out."

"Jesus, Cora was right." Nikki paced the short length of the living room. "You really don't know how to do a relationship. A part of me feels sorry for you."

Hey, I wasn't above her feeling sorry for me. She was at least feeling something for me. "I don't know how to fix this."

She threw her hands up in the air and stopped mid-pacing. "There's nothing you need to do because we weren't anything when I walked in on you. We didn't make promises to each other. So my head is telling me I can't be mad at you, my heart says I should tell you to get lost, and my body, well, my body sucks."

A smirk spread across my lips. "Your body does not suck, sugar."

She rolled her eyes and waved her hand in the air. "No, my body thinks it wants you."

I shook my head and grabbed her hand. "No, your body needs me, just like mine needs you."

"That may be true, but I can't think with only my body."

I pulled her close and wrapped my other arm around her waist. "Then how about you just feel with your body."

She closed her eyes and slightly shook her head. "I can't. Not yet."

"Yet?"

She opened her eyes and tilted her head back to look up at me. "Because the last time we did that, I ended up moving an hour away. I'm kind of fond of Kales Corners for the time being."

"Does that mean I need to leave?" Please Lord, don't say yes.

She bit her bottom lip, and her eyes shifted down. "Um, I guess you're okay living over there."

"But am I okay being here, right now?"

A smile spread across her lips, and she looked up. "Maybe a little too close."

I pressed a quick kiss to her forehead and took a step back. "Better?"

A laugh bubbled from her lips. "For now."

And the carefree, sexy angel I knew surfaced for two seconds when her eyes connected with mine. "Sugar, I love when you look at me like that."

She ducked her head. "Damn you," she whispered.

I was pushing her. She wanted me, and I wasn't going to let her run from it anymore. She had come to me that night to be with me, and I had been a dumbass by not recognizing it. "What are you guys up to tomorrow?" I wanted to push her, but not away from me.

"Um, I think Karmen mentioned driving to some state park nearby and having a picnic. I really don't know what she's thinking half of the time. Cora isn't into nature, and I don't think Karmen is up for hiking."

"Yeah, I can't really imagine you three traipsing through the woods with a picnic basket. I figured the mall would be more your speed."

Nikki ran her fingers through her hair and laughed. "Definitely more my thing. I'm more of a nature in small segments kind of girl. You know, while walking from my house to my car is a good bit of nature for me. But Karmen was all gung-ho about the park today, so who knows where we're going to end up." Nikki smothered a yawn with the back of her hand and sighed.

I brushed her hair back from her face. "I should let you get some sleep, sugar. Whatever you guys end up doing, you're going to need your strength."

"Um, are you going to come with us? You know, uh, well, because of Cora," she stuttered.

"Yeah, I suppose I should be there." Wrecker had told me I needed to keep a close eye on Cora, so the fact Nikki was going to be with her the whole time worked perfectly. "Knock on my door when you guys figure out what you're going to do."

She nodded and took another step back from me. I had pushed her far enough tonight. I got to touch her, and she hadn't flinched away. Definitely progress.

"See you in the morning, sugar." I slipped out the front door and waited 'til I heard the lock slip into place before I pulled a cigarette out and lit the end of it.

I may have spent the whole night with Nikki and her friends, but I found out she still wanted me. Even though she was fighting it, I knew she wanted me.

Fuck yeah.

*

Chapter 18

Nikki

"I don't want to leave. I'm going to tell Nickel I'm moving to Kales Corners. It's so peaceful here."

"Yeah, well, I'm pretty sure if you're not home in an hour, Nickel's going to come here, throw you over his shoulder, and never let you leave again."

Karmen tapped her chin. "The whole throwing me over his shoulder thing sounds pretty damn hot."

Cora slammed her door and rolled down the window. "Get in the car, woman. As much as I loved being here, I'm looking forward to sleeping in my own bed tonight, alone."

Karmen wrapped me up in a hug and whispered in my ear. "Call me whenever, okay? And make sure you give Pipe hell."

"Love you," I laughed.

"Love you too."

Cora waved as Karmen backed down the driveway, and Pipe came to stand next to me.

"Gonna miss them?" he asked.

"Yes and no."

"That's not the answer I expected."

"I'm going to miss them, of course, but I'm glad to have my house back to myself. Karmen can be a little exhausting at times."

Pipe nodded. "I can totally see that."

Karmen and Cora were gone, and now I had no idea what to do with Pipe. I knew he was only hanging out with us before because of Cora, and now that she was gone, to say this was awkward was an understatement.

"When do you go back to work?"

"Um." I shuffled my feet nervously and kicked a rock. "Tomorrow, twelve to eight."

"You like working there?"

I looked up at him. "It pays the bills. Can't really ask for much more."

"Can I ask a question?"

I really wish he wouldn't. I would much rather run into my house and hide 'til work tomorrow. I wasn't kidding when I said I was exhausted from this weekend. "Hit me with it. Can't make a promise I'll answer."

He pulled out a cigarette and held it between his fingers. "Am I wasting my time here?"

I cleared my throat and hitched my thumb over my shoulder. "I think I'm going to head into the house."

"Not gonna answer me, huh? I see how it is. You're gonna string me along then drop me like a sack of shit when you find a better deal."

I laughed and shook my head. "That's hardly what I'm doing, but if that's what you wanna think, that's fine."

"Then tell me what you're doing."

"Trying not to get hurt again. See ya later, Pipe." I walked back into the house, flipped the lock on the door, and leaned against it, sliding down to my butt.

Was that too harsh? Should I have told him he wasn't wasting his time?

I was terrified he was going to freak out if we hooked up, and then I would be back in the same spot again. I wanted to try, but dammit if the man didn't terrify me.

I scooted back, reached up to unlock the door, and swung it open. "Pipe," I called.

He spun around, still standing in the same spot I had left him. "Yeah, sugar? You okay?"

I had to look like a fool sitting on my ass opening the door. "Yeah, I'm fine. Just, uh, don't leave." I slammed the door shut and scrubbed my hands down my face.

God that was a fool thing to do, but if I didn't tell him I wanted him around, how was he going to know?

So, for now, he knew I didn't want him to leave. What I was going to do with him, I had no clue, but I at least knew he wasn't going anywhere soon.

*

Pipe

I wasn't going anywhere.

*

Chapter 19

Nikki

"Come over."

I rolled over on my back and looked at the time. "Alice, it's almost ten o'clock. I'm not coming over. I'm already in bed."

"But you sound sad."

I rolled my eyes and bounced out of bed. "I'm not sad, I'm just confused."

I hadn't talked to or seen Pipe since I told him not to leave. Not one single word. That was six days ago, and I was starting to wonder if he had packed up and left.

"Not sad, Alice."

"Well, whatever the hell you are, I don't like it. This man has got you all twisted up yet again."

I laughed and opened the fridge. "Maybe he's giving me space?"

Alice scoffed. "The man should be groveling at your feet every second. Have you talked to Karmen about it? Maybe she has seen him in Weston."

I grabbed the gallon of vanilla ice cream out of the freezer and a can of root beer. "I talked to her Tuesday, I think. She's busy at work and getting more pregnant by the day. She claims the baby is taking over her body."

"Well, maybe you should go over there. Say you're doing a welfare check."

I grabbed a spoon and pried the lid off the container of ice cream. "Um, what?"

"I've been watching too many cop shows lately, sorry. Just go over there and say hey. He'll take it from there."

I dropped two huge scoops into my cup. "Yeah, maybe some other time, Alice. I don't think he would appreciate that this late at night."

A flash of light startled me, and my eyes shot to the front window. "Oh, my God," I gasped.

I dropped the phone and ice cream scoop and backed further into the kitchen to the sliding door.

Someone was standing outside my house on the sidewalk, and I think they just took a picture of me. My heart raced, and I racked my brain trying to figure out what to do. I backed up to the sliding door, my hand gripping the handle and I slid it open far enough to slip out.

Pipe.

Pipe would help me.

My eyes scanned my back yard, my feet carrying over to Pipe's backdoor on their own accord.

I banged on the glass, whipping my head back and forth and making sure whoever was out front hadn't come around back.

"Pipe," I whispered. God, please, let him be home.

The light flipped on in the hallway, and my heart soared when he walked into the kitchen shirtless and running his fingers through his hair.

"Nikki, what the hell are you doing here?"

Jesus, my heart sank realizing those were the same words the last time I showed up at his house unannounced.

This was different, though. I was scared for a completely different reason that had nothing to do with him.

I put a hand on his muscled stomach and pushed him into the house. I slid the door shut behind me and twisted the lock. I looked up at him and gulped. "Someone is outside, and I think they were taking pictures of me."

Pipe tensed and twisted around to look out his front window. "Are you sure?"

"I'm sure there was someone watching me. I was in the kitchen talking to Alice, and I saw a flash from the window. I don't know what else it could have been except for someone taking a picture."

Pipe grabbed my arm and dragged me down the short hallway past the bathroom and straight into his bedroom. He reached into his dresser, pulled out a handgun, and tucked it in the back of his waistband. "Stay here. Don't move. If you hear anyone coming down this hallway, call nine-one-one."

Shit. "I don't have my phone. I dropped it."

Pipe pulled his from his pocket and thrust it into my hand. "Here. You hear anything weird, call the police."

I gripped his phone in my hand. "Where are you going? I think we should just call the police and let them handle this."

"Not gonna discuss this. Stay here, I'll holler when I'm coming so you know it's me." He disappeared from the room, glancing over his shoulder at me as he closed the door. "You're fine, sugar."

The door clicked shut behind him, and a whole new fear overtook my body. What if something happened to Pipe?

What if whatever wahoo who was outside had a gun too and managed to get a shot off before Pipe could? I sat down on the edge of his bed and stared at the door.

I checked the time on the phone and saw it had only been two minutes since I ran over to Pipe's. Freakin' hell.

I was on high alert listening for any noise, but the house was quiet.

Was that a good or bad sign?

Pipe's phone vibrated in my hand, and my name flashed on the screen. **At your place. You left the door open.**

Shit, I had. **Yeah. I was in a bit of a hurry.**

Just making sure. I'm headed back.

I moved to the bedroom door but didn't open it until I heard Pipe holler my name.

"Are you okay?" I called as I swung open the door and ran smack dab into Pipe.

He gripped my arms, steadying me. "I'm fine, sugar. You're the one I'm worried about." He handed me my phone. "Call back Alice. She called when I was putting the ice cream back in the freezer."

I looked down at my phone and handed him back his. "Thank you," I mumbled. I saw Alice had called six times and texted me more than ten.

"Oh, my God. Are you okay? I'm putting my shoes on, I'll be right over."

"What? No," I sputtered. "I'm fine. Well, at least now I am. I'm over at Pipe's."

"Wait, what? The last I heard from you was 'oh, my God,' and now you're over at Pipe's? What did I miss?"

I looked up at Pipe who was studying me. "Uh, well, I saw someone outside my house, and I came over to Pipe's because I was scared."

"Someone was outside of your house? Who the hell was it? Are you sure it wasn't Mrs. Stewart walking her dog?"

Pipe rolled his eyes and took the phone out of my hand and put it on speaker. "It wasn't an old lady with her dog. Nikki is fine right now. No need to come over in your cow pajamas, although that might help to scare them away."

"Hey," she protested. "I am not scary enough to scare the bad guys away, and how did you know I was wearing them? Who's spying on who, huh?"

Pipe shook his head. "Hanging up now, Alice. Nikki is fine. She'll call you in the morning." He ended the call before she could say anything else and handed the phone back to me. "Your girls all got a bit of crazy in them, don't they?"

I couldn't really deny that. I shrugged and put the phone back in my pocket. "They get all crazy because they care."

He grabbed my hand and tugged me down the hallway. He sat down on the couch, pulled me into his lap, and wrapped his arms around me. It felt nice to be in his arms. "I didn't find anyone outside, but I did find some fresh footprints in the dirt by your window."

"What?" I gasped. I pushed against his chest and pulled out of his arms. "Who was it?"

He ran his hand through his hair. "I don't know. By the time I got outside, they were gone."

I looked out his front window and shivered. Someone had been looking in my window, and I had no idea who it was. I looked down at Pipe. "What am I supposed to do?"

"You'll stay here tonight. There isn't much I can do right now. I'm gonna need you to think of anyone who might have done this."

"Don't you think we should call the police?"

He brushed back my hair. "We can if you want, sugar, but they aren't going to be able to do anything. There isn't anything out there besides a few footprints."

I sighed and closed my eyes. "Oh, my God."

"Just breath, sugar. Nothing is going to happen to you."

I opened my eyes. "And how do you know that?"

"Because I'm not letting you out of my sight until I get this shit figured out and take care of whoever this punk is."

"Pipe, you can't be with me every second of the day. You haven't been around this whole past week. How do expect to go from never being here to being glued to my side?"

"What are you talking about?"

I rolled my eyes and tried to slide off his lap, but he wrapped his arms around me again. "I know you haven't been around."

"Sugar," he drawled. "I don't leave for Weston until I know you are at work, and then I make sure I'm home before you get off work."

"What?" How did I not know that? "Do you like sitting in the dark all of the time?" There was never a light on at night at his place. That was why I assumed he was never home.

He chuckled and rubbed his hand up and down my back. "Now who's peeking into people's windows?"

I slugged him in the shoulder. "Totally not the same, ass."

"I got a fucked-up sleep schedule, sugar. So fucked up to the point where I sleep for a couple of hours while you're awake then I don't sleep 'til about six in the morning."

"Why the hell would you sleep like that?" Sleep was golden. There weren't many things that were better.

He shrugged his shoulders. "Got a lot of shit on my mind."

I tilted my head. "Sexy biker problems?"

He chuckled and shook his head. "I think that's the nicest thing you've said to me since I moved here."

I rolled my eyes. "Geez, don't let it go to your head, it might explode."

He leaned close, his hand pressing me closer. "Although I have to say, you telling me not to leave were the two sweetest words I had ever heard."

I bit my lip, and my eyes slid to my lap.

His hand reached up and tipped back my chin. "Those two words said a lot."

"I...I..." Not a damn clue what to say.

"So does the fact you were looking for me all week mean you were hoping I was going to come over?"

I cleared my throat. "Don't you think we should talk about the guy who was outside my house?"

Pipe shook his head. "I know you're safe. I grabbed your soda and ice cream and put it in your fridge and locked up your house, and I know nothing is going to happen to you when I'm with you, so I think we're talking about the right thing."

Danger, Will Robinson.

I looked around his living room realizing his side was just like mine, except not nearly updated as mine was. "What is that on the floor?" A huge, brown stain was on the gray carpet.

"I try not to think about it, and always have my shoes on."

I looked down at my bare feet. "I just walked around on your carpet. The hallway and bedroom aren't as bad as this."

"I don't really think that is as reassuring as you think it is," I mumbled. "How are you even living here?"

Part of the drywall by the front door was crumbling, and the pink insulation was peeking out. The only nice things in the living room were the couch we were sitting on, and the TV that was hanging on the wall. "They don't even have trim on the floors."

Pipe shrugged. "They got me with the good location."

I rolled my eyes and turned my gaze to the kitchen. "Pipe, half of those cabinets don't even have doors on them."

"Yeah. They seem to be ripped off of the hinges," he said nonchalantly.

"And you pay rent for this place?"

"Yeah, and they even had me pay a deposit."

My jaw dropped. "For what? This place is a dump."

"Don't hold back, sugar," Pipe chuckled. "It's a place to lay my head down at night."

I wrinkled my nose. "Well, don't stub your toe or anything, and make sure you get a tetanus shot."

"What does stubbing my toe have to do with anything?"

I shrugged. "I don't know. It's just something I wouldn't do here."

He brushed my hair from my neck. "Thanks for looking out for me, sugar," he whispered.

My cheeks heated, and I leaned into his body. "Um, well, you did help me tonight."

"So you feel obligated to care about me?" He leaned closer, and his breath floated across my skin.

"No," I gasped.

"Then what do you feel?"

My head swam with his scent of tobacco, leather, and musk. Most people who smoked carried a heavy scent of smoke with them, but with Pipe, it was different. "Um, what do I feel?" I asked dumbly.

"For me, Nikki."

I gulped and turned my head. My eyes connected with his, and I bit my lip.

"Fuck it," he growled. His hands moved from my waist and delved into my hair. His lips crashed down on mine, and a moan was ripped from my lips. I twisted in his lap, my hands resting on his shoulders.

I pressed down on his shoulders, lifted my body up, my lips never leaving his, and parted my legs to straddle him.

"Jesus Christ, sugar," he growled against my lips. I squeezed my legs around him, and his hands traveled down my back, and he palmed my ass. "Fucking missed this, sugar."

I mewled against his lips and opened my mouth. His tongue plunged into my mouth, and I threaded my fingers through his hair. His fingers dug into my ass and pressed me flush against his body.

He stood up, lifting me in his arms, and walked toward the bedroom. "Where are we going?" I whispered.

"Somewhere more comfortable," he muttered. He pushed open the door to the bedroom and laid me down in the middle of the bed.

He looked down at me, his eyes dark with desire. "Pipe, please." I didn't know what I was pleading for, but I wanted it. I wanted Pipe. All of him.

"You sure, sugar?"

I nodded my head and half sat up, resting back on my elbows. "I want you."

His hands went to button on his jeans, and he popped it open. "You may think you want me, sugar, but I know you're like me. You need me."

I wasn't going to admit that. Needing was a whole level above wanting. "Did anyone ever tell you, you talk too much?"

"Did anyone ever tell you, you avoid shit way too much?"

"If by shit you mean anything to do with you and me, then yes, yes I do." My brain was less likely to explode when I didn't try to figure out what I wanted from Pipe. "But I am going to point out you just admitted to needing me." Which was huge. My heart tried to beat out of my chest as he slid the zipper down on his jeans.

"Not gonna hide it, sugar. I may have fucked up with you the first time, but now that I've got a second chance and you're in my bed, all my cards are out on the table."

"And what exactly do those cards say?" I whispered.

He slid his pants down his legs and stepped out of them. "I'm here," he said as he put one knee on the bed. "I'm yours." His other knee pressed into the bed, and his hands touched my legs. "I'm not leaving 'til you give us a chance."

I jack-knifed off the bed, coming up on my knees, and wrapped my arms around his neck. "Say it again," I whispered against his lips.

I felt his lips slide into a smile. "I'm yours."

"I have to admit. I didn't think you were going to actually come to your senses. Cora said it might take years."

"Cora's been around the club life too long and thinks she knows everything. I knew the day you disappeared, I had fucked up." He trailed his fingertips up my arms. "I'm the one who should be saying I thought this would take much longer. I figured I had a lot of groveling left to do."

I pressed my lips against his ear. "Oh, you're not done groveling yet. It's only just begun."

He growled low, wrapped his arms around me, and swept me off my knees. He pressed my body close to his and dropped me down onto the bed with his body covering mine. "You haven't seen nothing yet, sugar." His hands moved to the waistband of my leggings and tugged them down while his lips assaulted my neck, kissing, licking, and nipping his way down my body.

"Sugar, as much as these pants looking fucking amazing on you, they are a fucking pain in the ass to get off you."

I giggled as he got them to my calves and had to sit back on his knees to take them off one leg at a time. "Don't knock my leggings. I have a rather unhealthy obsession with buying them. You might want to rethink about dating me because I might swipe your credit card and go on a shopping spree."

He tossed the leggings over his shoulder and covered me with his body again. "I'm pretty sure that's a habit I can support if it makes your ass look that fucking good."

"You were checking out my ass?"

"Nikki, there isn't a time when I'm around you I'm not checking out your ass."

I laughed and wrapped my arms around his shoulders. "You're such a man."

"Pretty sure that's what you like about me, sugar."

"I think I might need to be acquainted with the man side of you. It's been a while." Damn Pipe had broken me for any other man. As in, if they weren't Pipe, I didn't want them.

He grabbed the hem of my shirt, tugged it up my body, and I leaned into him so he could pull it over my head. His hands formed to the cups of my bra, and he gently squeezed. "Does that mean you forgot our night together?"

I shook my head and trailed my fingertips up his arms. "Pretty sure that night will forever be burned into my memory."

He pressed a kiss to my lips. "That night alone has gotten me through the past month without you."

My body froze, and I hit him on the chest. "Let me up."

"Wait, what?"

"I said let me up. I don't want to be in your bed, and you lie to me." I struggled against him, and he grabbed my arms, moving them over my head.

"What the hell just happened?" he demanded.

"What happened was you said the thought of you and me got you through the past month when I know you had women in your bed that replaced me."

"Who the fuck told you that?" he barked. His eyes darkened again, but this time I know, it wasn't passion he was feeling. He was pissed off.

"No one told me that because I saw it with my own eyes." I didn't have any grand illusions Pipe had pined away for me. I had seen with my own eyes what he was doing when I wasn't around.

"You think that I fucked around this whole month, Nikki? How the fuck did you figure that?" His grip tightened on my wrists, and he pulled my arms taut above my head.

I strained against his hold, but I knew he wasn't going to let me go. "Because it took you a whole month to find me. If you really wanted me, you would have been knocking down my door before I even left. I came to your room, saw you with that chick, and then you let me leave."

"I didn't fucking let you do anything. You left because instead of telling me what the hell you were feeling, you ran with your tail between your legs. I didn't fucking know what was going on with us. You were there, and then you were gone."

"I didn't know what else to do."

He leaned down, his lips hovering over mine. "And I didn't know what to do either. But I've figured it out, and I'm not going to let you push me away for some bullshit reason. You weren't the first chick to show up at my door, but you were the first to make me feel like a jackass."

I ground my teeth. "Sorry I wasn't able to stroke your ego."

"So fucking sassy," he growled. "I'm gonna clue you in on something, and you're not going to like it, but you need to get past whatever bullshit feelings you have and listen."

"You're not really giving me much choice." I tried one last time to yank my arms down, but he wasn't budging.

"I have been with a shit ton of women, Nikki."

"Duh," I scoffed. I would have to be an idiot not to know that.

"And each one always came back, wanting more."

I bucked my hips and shook my head. "Nope, don't wanna know this."

"Shush, woman. That's the part you're going to have to get over. They all came back for more, but none of them got it. I wasn't interested in more than one night, and that was it. It didn't matter who they were"

"Then I guess I better go," I muttered.

"I didn't want them again because they didn't offer me anything I couldn't get from ten other women. Then you happened. Your smart mouth and sexy body found their way into my bed, and for the first fucking time, I wanted more."

"Well, you had a shitty way of showing me you wanted more." A woman in his bed wasn't the best way to show me that.

"As soon you walked away from me that night, I kicked that chick out of my bed. All I could think about this past month was you and me that night. All I wanted was that night over, and as much I would have liked to move on from you and take any chick to bed with me, the only one that would do was you. Fucking A, Nikki. I tried, one night I got so fucking desperate, hating the fact that you had left, I tried to be with someone else. It didn't fucking work because the only way I could get hard was to close my eyes and think of you. I tossed her out on her ass so quick because it felt like I was cheating on you even though there wasn't anything going on with us."

"So I'm supposed to be glad you tried to fuck me out of your system."

Pipe ran his fingers through his hair and rolled off me. "Nikki, you frustrate the hell out of me. You aren't listening to the parts that are important. I didn't have sex with anyone else because all I fucking want is you."

I clamped my mouth shut and turned my head to the side.

"So now you're not going to talk to me? Not letting you run again, Nikki. I'll keep telling you until you get it through your thick skull." He brushed my hair off my face and pressed a kiss to my neck.

Don't budge, Nikki. Do not bend to this man's touch.

*

Chapter 20

Pipe

Her soft skin beneath my lips reminded me why I was willing to fight for this woman 'til my last breath.

I knew she felt it, but she was too damn stubborn to admit it. "Talk to me, sugar. I don't know what's going on in that pretty little head of yours."

"It was a thick skull a minute ago," she grumbled.

"Even then, it was still pretty. Now talk," I insisted.

A sigh escaped from her lips. "We've talked about everything. Now it comes to the doing part, and I'm downright terrified."

I wiggled my eyebrows. "Doing part? You mean sex? Because you don't have anything to worry with that, sugar."

She socked me on the shoulder and rolled her eyes. "The part where we actually become an us. Where I'm the only person you're with."

"Don't know if you heard me before, but I've been doing that for the past month, I'm good."

She reached up and brushed her fingertips against my cheek. "But how long will you be good for? You just said you don't go back to the same girl twice. How do you know I'm going to be enough?"

"Sugar, the only way you're going to know if you are enough for me, is to just let go. You keep doubting every word coming out of my mouth, we'll be over before we even begin."

She closed her eyes, and her teeth snagged her bottom lip.

I held my breath knowing this was it. If she said no and didn't give me a second chance, we were done. I wasn't going to pressure her. She needed to come to her decision on her own. I had let her know everything she needed to know.

"Just promise me if you need to go, just let me know. Don't cheat on me or start resenting me. I can't handle that, Pipe. Just go if you need to."

"Open your eyes, sugar."

Her eyes slowly opened, and they were clouded with tears. "I've always been yours, Pipe."

My breath whooshed out of me, and I hung my head. "Fucking hell, woman. You know how to get right to the truth and gut me."

"I don't want to play games, Pipe," she whispered.

I dropped down on my elbows and nuzzled her neck. "Except the dick match game with your girls."

She giggled and tilted her head, giving me better access. "Except that."

I nipped her earlobe and whispered, "I need you right now, sugar."

She wrapped her arms around me. "I don't know what you're waiting for."

I chuckled and trailed kisses down her neck and over her exposed collarbone. "Not a damn thing. I'm not waiting for a damn thing anymore. I've got you again, and this time, I'm not letting you go."

Her nails scratched up my back. "Then take me," she whispered.

I didn't need to be told twice.

My legs tangled with hers, my hands gently grabbing her arms, and I flipped us over. My fingers unsnapped her bra, dragging the straps down her arms, and I tossed it on the floor. "God damn, Nikki," I growled. Her breasts were fucking perfect, gently hanging in front of me. "I've decided you aren't allowed to ever leave my bed. Naked twenty-four seven only for me." My hands molded to her breasts, and she leaned into my touch.

"As long as you're naked with me," she moaned.

My dick strained against the tight fabric of my boxers as my hands traveled around to her back and to her panties. "Not naked enough though," I mumbled. I worked her panties down her legs as far as I could, and she shimmied them off the rest of the way, rubbing her body against me the whole way.

She sat back, resting her hands on her bare thighs, and looked down at me.

I sat up and wrapped my arms around her waist. "I fucking missed this. One night, and you completely changed my world."

"You're welcome," she smirked. Her hands cradled my face. "We haven't even started yet, handsome."

Here was the Nikki who had caught my attention. Sexy as fuck, and sassy as hell. "Take my boxers off, sugar."

Her hands went to the waistband of my boxers, and I lifted up as she tugged them down. "Now we're talking," she muttered. Her fingers wrapped around my rock-hard dick, and she stroked up and down. "I think they're going to have to update that game and add The Pipe."

"Nah, that is just for you." I threaded my fingers through her hair, tugged her head to mine, and kissed the hell out of her.

Every time I missed her, I wondered where she was, and wished I could kiss her, I poured all that into this kiss. I pulled her down on top of me, our legs tangled, and our hands roamed each other's body.

"Pipe," she moaned as my hand snaked down between us, straight to her sweet cunt.

"Talk to me, sugar." I needed to hear every little moan, sigh, and word she had to say. I knew her body wanted me, but I needed to know what she was thinking. Getting into her head was my ultimate goal.

I stroked her clit, and my tongue glided through her mouth. Her moans surrounded me as she ground her pussy into my hand, demanding more.

"Stop, please," she gasped.

My hand stilled, and our eyes connected. Oh hell. "Nikki?" Please God, don't let her change her mind. I think my dick is going to explode if she doesn't let me fuck the hell out of her.

"I wanna come on your dick, not your hand."

And right then and there, I could have died a happy man.

This woman was fucking amazing. I slipped my hand from her sweet pussy and gripped her hip. "God, I was a fucking fool for ever letting you leave my bed before."

She pressed a kiss to my cheek. "We all make mistakes. It's all about how you fix them."

I flipped her over, sat back on my calves and looked down at her as I stroked my dick. "Lay back and watch me fix it, sugar."

She spread her legs and put her hands over her head. "Now that sounds like a plan."

My fingers found her clit while I stroked my dick up and down. "You remember that night, sugar? It was like your body was made for me. Every night, I relived that night, wishing you were with me again."

"Is that why you're stroking your cock instead of fucking me? That's what you're used to."

My hand left her body, and I grabbed her hips, pulling her closer to me. "I'm about to fuck that sass out of you, sugar."

"Promises, promises," she gasped as I plunged into her.

I caged her in with my arms, resting them next to her head, and slid in and out of her wet pussy. "Fucking made for me," I growled.

"Yes, oh God, yes," she moaned. She wound her arms around my neck and closed her eyes.

"You feel it, sugar? You feel that?"

"Yes, yes," she chanted over and over.

I felt it.

I fucking felt it everywhere.

I don't know how I could have been such a fool to think I could live without this or find it with some other woman.

Nikki was it for me.

She made me complete when I didn't even know I was missing something.

Her body responded to every touch and caress as my hands roamed over her. My dick plunged into her sweet cunt, milking me with each thrust.

I poured my cum into her while her body trembled beneath me as she found her sweet release.

"Good golly."

I collapsed to the side and pulled her into my arms. "Good golly, huh? Guess I'll have to try for a 'gosh darn' next time."

She burrowed into my arms and sighed. "Shut it," she mumbled. "You rendered me stupid for a bit. That's all I could think of."

I reached for the covers that had gotten kicked to the bottom of the bed and pulled them over us. "I'll take it, sugar, as long as you're lying naked in my bed."

"Pretty sure my legs aren't working right now, so even if you wanted to kick me out of your bed, you would have to carry me back to my place."

"One sec." I slipped from the bed, flipped off the lights, and climbed back into bed. "Sleep."

"Hmm, not going to argue with you on that one." She pressed a kiss to the underside of my chin and laid her head down on my shoulder. "Goodnight, handsome," she whispered into the dark.

Her breathing evened out, and I knew she was asleep.

In my arms.

In my bed.

Hallel-fuckin-ujah.

*

Chapter 21

Nikki

Ew.

"Pipe."

What the hell was I going to do? It was half past six, and what I planned on doing was going to the bathroom and then falling back into bed with Pipe. But his bathroom was hindering me from even stepping foot near the toilet.

"Sugar?" he called sleepily.

"Um, I can't do this."

"Oh hell," he mumbled. I turned, saw the light turn on in the bedroom, and he walked toward me naked. Beautifully naked. "Don't go in there."

I ripped my eyes off his dick that was at half-mast. "Yeah, I'm totally fine with that, except I really need to go to the bathroom.

"Can you make it next door?"

I looked down at my naked body. "Yeah, except I really don't want to do that naked."

"Grab one of my shirts, and we can go over there."

"We?" I asked.

Pipe turned around and headed back into his bedroom. "Not letting you go over there by yourself. You forget there was some creeper looking in your window eight hours ago?"

I had. "Thanks for the reminder," I mumbled. He tossed a shirt at me when I walked into the room, and I pulled it over my head. "Are we coming back over here?"

Pipe grabbed his boxers off the floor and tugged them on. "It's up to you, sugar. Your place is a hell of a lot nicer."

Thank God he had said it. "We can stay at my place. I can make breakfast when we wake up."

Pipe pulled out another shirt, a pair of pants, and socks. He grabbed my hand and pulled me down the hallway. "You mean when you wake up again. I'm ready to start the day."

I wrinkled my nose. "Are you insane?"

He laughed and slid open the patio door. "No, just don't sleep a lot."

I hummed under my breath and slipped out the door. "We're gonna have to change that."

"I think you already have. I just slept six hours. That's pretty damn good for me."

"Oh, well, you're welcome. Although I can tell you right now, as soon as I hit the bathroom, I'm falling back into bed." Any time before eight o'clock was not for me.

He opened the door to my house and motioned for me to go in. "Whatever you want, sugar."

Everything looked normal in my place, but it felt off. It felt like someone was watching me. "Um, where are you going to be while I try to sleep?"

"Here."

I licked my lips and looked down the hallway. "Here, as in bed next to me?"

He chuckled and shook his head. "No, I planned on making a pot of coffee and watching TV until you woke up."

I looked up at him and grimaced. "Um, I'll try to sleep on the couch."

He reached up and cupped my cheek. "Talk to me, sugar. Not even a minute ago, you were ready to pass out, and now you look like you've seen a ghost."

I glanced out the front window and shivered. "It feels like he's still there."

Pipe looked over his shoulder at the window and shook his head. He grumbled under his breath about perverts and skinning them alive. He stalked to the window and pulled the curtain closed. "He's not here, sugar, and I am. You have nothing to worry about."

"See, I know that in theory, but I'm still terrified."

He grabbed my hand and pulled me to the bathroom. He pushed me in and closed the door. "I'll be right here."

In any other circumstance, that would have been super weird, but right now, it made me feel safe. I did my business, washed my hands, and looked in the mirror where I promptly let out a scream.

"Nikki," Pipe called as he pulled open the door.

"How are you even looking at me right now without cringing?" I demanded. I grabbed my brush from the sink and pulled it through my hair. "Turn around."

Pipe chuckled and leaned against the doorframe. "I just looked at you for the past fifteen minutes."

I wrinkled my nose and turned back to the mirror. "Don't blame me if you have nightmares tonight."

"Not likely." He grabbed the brush from my hand and tossed it on the counter. "You look beautiful, Nikki. Knock it off." He pulled me from the bathroom and into the bedroom. "Shirt on or off?"

I looked up at him. "Huh?"

"You sleep naked or in the shirt? Although, I have to tell you, if you take that shirt off, we're fucking before you sleep."

I put my hands on my hips. "That is about the only thing that could ever compete with sex."

"So what's it gonna be, sugar?"

A smile spread across my lips, and I pulled the shirt over my head. "How's that for an answer, handsome?"

*

Pipe

"You're a liar."

I cracked one eye open. Nikki was leaning over me, her hair cascading down around us, and she had a huge smile on her face.

Now, this is how I could wake up every day. "You're like a fucking angel."

A blush crept up her cheeks. "We're talking about you, not me. You were sleeping."

I reached up and pulled her down for a kiss. "Yeah, I was," I mumbled against her lips.

"You said you don't sleep much." She threw a leg over my waist, straddling me. "You wanna tell me why that is? I know you said before you have a lot on your mind, but I think there's more to it than that."

"Trying to get in my head, sugar?"

She shrugged and sat back on my thighs. "Only if you want me there, handsome."

"You keep calling me that."

She stuck out her tongue. "That's 'cause I can't call you pretty."

"You're a goofball."

She shook her finger at me. "You're changing the subject. Tell me why you don't sleep much."

I sighed and fluffed the pillow under my head. "It's nothing big, sugar."

"I think the fact you can only sleep for a couple hours at a time is a rather big deal."

"I mean the reason why I don't sleep much isn't a big one."

"Then spill."

I rested my hands on her bare thighs and looked up at her. "I just was afraid people wouldn't be there when I woke up. I had this foster home when I was about eleven that I really liked. I went to sleep without a care in the world and woke up with my bag packed and I was out the door in my pajamas."

"But that wasn't your fault, Pipe. Staying awake all night wouldn't have changed anything."

"I know that now, but I still can't sleep much."

She sighed and rested her hands on top of mine. "But you did just sleep for six hours and then again for three."

"I think that might have to do a bit with the workout you put me through."

She ran her fingers up my arms and planted her hands on my chest. "Then I guess I need to work you out every night so you can get a good night's sleep."

"Is that a threat?"

A smile spread across her lips. "More like a promise. A promise I'm going to fulfill right now."

*

Chapter 22

Nikki

"I gotta run to Weston for the day."

"Oh, okay."

Pipe drank the rest of his coffee and set it on the counter. "Don't look at me like that, sugar. I haven't been there since last week."

I rolled my eyes and grabbed his empty cup. "I know. We've kind of been in our own bubble the past few days. I can't really expect to keep you all to myself."

He grabbed my hand and pulled me around the counter. He turned, spreading his legs, and tucked me in between them.

"Hey, no hankie pankie on the clock," Bos called from the window.

"You really think he has to say that every time I touch you?"

I put my hands on Pipe's shoulders and sighed. "At least there isn't anyone close when he yelled it this time. I swear, Mrs. Sawyer about had a heart attack yesterday when she turned around and saw your hand on my butt."

"Hey, she should have been happy she got a show with her meal." His hands went to my butt like they did every morning, and he gently squeezed. "We have a much smaller crowd today. Miller and Steve haven't even looked up from their coffee yet, and I'm pretty sure Maury is sleeping."

"You keeping tabs on everyone now?"

"Gotta keep you safe, sugar. Now kiss me so I can sort out Wrecker's shit and be back here before you clock out."

I leaned down and pressed a quick kiss to his lips. "If you're not back in time, I'll just have Bos give me a ride home."

"I'll be here. The only person you're getting a ride home from is me. Although, I did tell Bos to keep an eye on you until I got back."

"Oh good, now I'll have him watching my every move. At least with you, I was able to distract you."

He pulled a cigarette out of his pocket and stuck it in the corner of his mouth. I snatched it away and tucked it into my apron "Hey, give that back."

I shook my head and pulled out of his arms. "Nope, I've decided you need to quit."

He rolled his eyes and patted his pocket. "Good luck with that, sugar. I've got a full pack in here. You can keep that one to remind you of me while I'm gone."

I lunged for his pocket, but he turned away and slipped out of his chair. "Behave while I'm gone, and try not to give Bos too much hell."

He snagged me around the neck, pulling me close for a quick, heated kiss and then he was out the door before I could even think.

"You two are so darn cute together." Alice breezed into the cafe and sat down in the chair Pipe had just been in. "I saw you two from the window, and I'm pretty sure a car passing by heard me sigh."

I set Pipe's empty cup in the window for Bos to take and sat down next to Alice. "And just what are you doing here? It's your day off. If I were you, I would still be sleeping."

Alice shook her head. "No, if you were me, you would still be in bed, but you wouldn't be sleeping." She wiggled her eyebrows and grabbed a menu.

"Um, you really need to look at a menu?" I laughed.

"Hey, I want to feel like an actual customer today. Maybe be a little difficult and send my food back to Bos a few times."

"Try it, and I'll add a special ingredient every time," he called from the window.

Alice rolled her eyes. "I swear, that man has bionic ears," she mumbled. "Man, we really do have a lot of shit on the menu, don't we?"

"There's a lot, but most of the people order the same thing, so Bos only makes about ten things off a menu that has thirty things."

Alice smiled and pointed her finger at something on the menu. "When do you think was the last time Bos made Eggs Benedict?"

"Not happening," he called.

"Oh, come on," Alice protested. "It's on the damn menu. What happened to the customer always being right?"

Bos stood in front of the window and pointed his spatula at Alice. "You're getting a ham and cheese omelette, home fries, sourdough toast, and bacon."

Alice shrugged. "I guess that'll do."

Bos rolled his eyes and moved his pointing spatula at me. "You tell your biker about Richard?"

"Richard?" Alice asked. "What do you need to tell Pipe about him?"

"He asked her out, and I think he's got something weird going on in his head about Nikki."

I scoffed and moved to the coffeepot. "Richard is harmless. I didn't tell Pipe about him, but I will tonight. It's Wednesday so Pipe can see him when he picks me up." The more I thought about Richard trying to hurt me, the more I realized Bos was crazy for thinking Richard was infatuated with me.

"Backup, backup," Alice insisted. "I have heard nothing about Richard and you. Spill."

"He asked her out," Bos called. "She told him no, but did it in a way that made it sound like she was interested."

"Girl, you need to shut that shit down right now. I'm sure Bos has heard the same rumors I have. Richard is a few donuts short of a dozen." Alice twirled her finger by her ear and stuck her tongue out. "I'd stay far away from him if he's interested in you."

Now Alice was warning me about Richard. "Look, I think you are both wrong, but like I said, Pipe can meet him tonight. and if he says the same thing you guys are, then we'll have to close the diner and move it."

Bos grunted. "More like we'll have to fire your ass, and you'll need to move back to Weston."

"What?" Alice gasped. "You're moving back to Weston?"

I rolled my eye and grabbed her a clean cup. "I don't know. Pipe and I have only been actually together for a week. I think that's a little too soon to jump the gun. I'm happy in Kales Corners right now, and as far as I know, so is Pipe."

"Well, I guess you're right. But you better promise you'll tell me when you're leaving, and you'll have to come visit at least once a month."

"I feel like this is kind of like a custody arrangement," I mumbled. I filled her coffee cup and wandered over to the other two tables to see if they needed a refill.

Bos had her food done in record time, and I set it down in front of her. I sat back down next to Alice and stole a piece of bacon off her plate. "What are your plans today?"

Alice buttered her toast and shoved half a piece into her mouth. "Mah, tin my van."

I tilted my head and took a bite of bacon. "How strange is it I actually know what you just said? Mall and then some Vin."

Alice touched her nose and nodded her head. "Ding, ding," she gasped as she swallowed. "Jesus, could you dry out the toast a little bit more, Bos, I just about choked on it."

"Don't put the whole damn piece in your mouth, and it won't be a problem," he grumbled.

"Old man is going to be the death of me," Alice mumbled. "So, what are you doing after work besides Pipe?" She elbowed me in the side and wiggled her eyebrows.

I rolled my eyes. "Not much. We've just been hanging out around the house lately."

"You wanna go to The Bar tonight? They have dice and pull tabs tonight."

"I thought you hated going to The Bar. Now you wanna actually hang out there voluntarily?"

She shrugged and shoveled in a fork full of eggs. "It'll be fun, and we can play a couple games of pool."

It actually sounded like fun, and I knew Pipe would be cool with it too. "If that'll get you away from Vin for a night, then I'm down with it."

I pulled out my phone, knowing Pipe was driving, but he would get the message when he got to Weston.

We were going to make our first public appearance as a couple. I was nervous, but a whole lot excited.

*

Chapter 23

Pipe

"Listen up," Wrecker called. He slammed his gavel down and looked at each of us. "Shut the hell up, Maniac."

Maniac stroked his beard and nodded at Wrecker. "Sorry, brother."

Wrecker grunted. "Just shut your mouth, and you won't have to be sorry. We got some shit to talk about."

"This about Cora?" Nickel asked.

"Sure as fuck is. The more chicks we get around here, the more I wanna rip my fucking hair out." Wrecker dropped the gavel on the table and scrubbed his hands down his face. "She's got a friend."

"Friend?" Maniac asked. "She can stay in my room," he laughed.

The guys chuckled, and Wrecker slammed his hand down on the table. "Yuck it up, dumbasses, but we got some shit to discuss. Cora wants her friend to fucking live at the clubhouse. Apparently, she's gotten into some shit, and she's struggling to get out of it."

"What kind of shit?" I asked.

"The kind that can get you a bullet in the back of your head. She was dating a guy from a rival club, they broke up, and now she knows some shit she shouldn't."

"What club?" Nickel asked.

"Hell Captains."

"Them again," Brinks scoffed. "I'm not the one who's going to talk to them. They're half-baked and a bunch of dumbasses."

"Well, her friend didn't realize they were a bunch of dumbasses until too late. Now they want her dead because she knows shit only members should know."

"Well, how the hell does she know shit? Her dumbass boyfriend tell her stuff?" Maniac asked.

Wrecker nodded.

"Power of the pussy," Slayer laughed. "Bet that guy got a taste, and he opened his mouth too much."

That was probably exactly what happened. Now the guy was probably off scot-free, and now Cora's friend was going to have to pay.

"What's her name?" Slayer asked.

"Wren. I haven't told Cora yes or no. I had first said that maybe Wren should go stay with her brother, but Cora said there was no way that was going to happen."

Slayer leaned forward in his chair and rested his elbows on the table. "You ever stop to think why Cora isn't a fan of her own brother?"

"Because he's an asshole. We all know that," Nickel laughed.

"What do you guys think of Wren staying at the clubhouse until her shit blows over?" Wrecker asked the room.

Brinks cleared his throat. "You really think this is going to blow over? You know if she comes in here, we're going to be the ones who takes care of her problem for her."

"That's why I brought it to the table. Dealing with getting away from the River Valley bullshit and now adding in Cora's friend means we're gonna have double the bullshit to deal with." Wrecker flattened his hands on the table. "Her friend is going to need to have someone on her twenty-four seven. Meaning, one of you is either going to have to volunteer, or I'm gonna make one of you do it."

Everyone shifted in their chairs and looked at anything but Wrecker.

Wrecker looked at me, and I shook my head. No way in hell was I going to be Wren's keeper. I had plans of moving back to Weston and spending all of my time in bed with Nikki.

"Jesus," Maniac cried. "I'll do it. How hard can it be?"

"Famous last words," Nickel chuckled. "You ever had a woman for more than a few hours?" he asked.

Maniac flipped him off. "Not interested in that bull shit, man. I plan on keeping this chick in her room. From where I'm sitting, I've got a pretty easy job. You fuckers can deal with Jenkins and the Hell Captains."

"You're a dumbass, Maniac, but you can find out on your own how screwed you are. She's friends with Cora, so you have to assume she's going to be just like her," Brinks laughed.

"Really?" Maniac asked, suddenly doubting his decision. "I want a redo."

"Not a fucking chance," Clash laughed. "Wren is all yours."

"All right, now that is taken care of, we need to talk about River Valley. Jenkins called and asked us to make a run next week to California."

"You're fucking kidding me."

"Is he insane?"

"Bull fucking shit."

Nickel stood up and looked down at Wrecker. "This is fucking bullshit. It's one thing making these runs around here, but now he wants us to cross five states with this shit strapped to the back of our bikes? Fuck him."

"I'll be making the run myself. I'm not going to put you guys on the line like that." He crossed his arms over his chest. "That's not an issue. What we need to talk about is what we are doing to get the hell away from this shit. You find anything out about who Jenkins made a deal with, Brinks?"

"Oakley Mykel. He is the guy behind The Ultra."

"What in the fuck is The Ultra?" Maniac asked.

Brinks shook his head and pulled out his phone. "Exactly who I had hoped wasn't involved in this, but they are." He swiped a couple of times and flipped his phone around for us to see. "This is Oakley Mykel. A notorious drug dealer that is well known all over the US."

"What's he so notorious for?" Slayer asked.

"For getting the job done no matter what. Right now, the unofficial head count of people who got in his way and are no longer around is well over one hundred."

Wrecker whistled low. "Jesus. I've never heard of the guy, but when we're not into the drug deals and only into the muling, I guess we don't need to know those details."

"So how hard is it to get near this guy and get a meeting with him?" I asked.

"From what I've gathered from the surface, that is near to impossible. Our best chance of getting near him is to run into him accidentally."

"What do you mean accidentlly?" Wrecker asked.

"Like a decoy," Boink chimed in.

"That could work," Brinks muttered. "I'm not sure who we could use and what they could be, but it's something to consider."

"Who does he have around him?" Wrecker asked. "Does he have an ol' lady?"

Brinks had his nose buried in his phone. "From what I can find, he has a kid, but there doesn't appear to be a mom or wife in sight."

"Find out if he's attached to anyone. The easiest way to get to any guy is through his dick. I might know a chick who's looking for money that would fit the bill perfectly to try to get close to Oakley"

We all looked at Wrecker, half of us with our jaws dropped. "You know a woman?" Boink asked.

Jesus. We were all thinking the same thing, but leave it to Boink to say it out loud. Wrecker was unlike your typical biker. He didn't sleep around, and he was rarely ever around anyone who wasn't part of the club. We all assumed he had something going on the side, but none of us had the balls to ask him.

Wrecker grabbed the gavel and smashed it down on the table. "Find out if he's with anyone. If not, let me know." He strolled out of the room and slammed the door shut behind him.

"Well, that was unexpected. I thought the man was a monk," Slayer chuckled.

"Or gay," Boink added.

"Now that I never thought," Nickel laughed.

I rolled my eyes and pushed away from the table. "I'd worry more about Cora's friend coming and Oakley than who Wrecker has in his bed."

Maniac scoffed and put his head in his hands. "Why did I volunteer to do this? Maybe you should do it, Nickel. You got Karmen all figured out."

Nickel shook his head. "Not fucking happening. Karmen is the only chick I signed up for. Wren is all yours, brother."

"I'd advise not messing around with her though because she's Cora's friend, and I don't know about anyone else, but that chick terrifies me." Slayer shivered and grimaced. "She's hot, but man, she has got a mouth on her. Pretty sure the chick would argue with the wall if she didn't like the paint color."

"Well, then it's a good thing Maniac has to deal with her, and you have to help Brinks with the Oakley shit." I stuck a cigarette in the corner of my mouth and flipped my lighter over in my hand. "I am gonna put the bike up and grab my truck before I head back to Kales Corners."

"You're going back? I thought for sure when Karmen told me you two hooked up that you would be back here last week."

I pushed in my chair and shrugged. "I'm leaving that up to Nikki. I don't mind the ride back and forth, although with it cooling down and the snow coming soon, it would be nicer to be closer to the clubhouse." Having to park the bike every winter was a bummer, but with being so far away, I was parking it a bit sooner than normal because a two-way ride every day in forty degree weather tended to chill me to the bone by the time I got to the club or home.

"So you get to leave, and we have to stay here and figure shit out. Not fucking fair," Slayer complained.

"Yeah, well, when you become VP, you can do that shit. I'll see you fuckers later. Try not to drive Wrecker crazy." Lord knows the man had enough shit on his plate right now, he didn't need anything else distracting him.

I made it to the end of the hallway and ran into Wrecker who was walking out of his room. "You leaving?"

"I was gonna put the bike up and pull out my truck. That'll take me a couple of hours, and then I'll be gone. Did you need me to do anything?"

Wrecker shook his head. "Nah, I'm good. I got some shit to take care of outside of the clubhouse today. The guys hopefully shouldn't blow up the place? while I'm gone."

I chuckled and ran my fingers through my hair. "Gotta cut 'em some slack. Brinks will keep them in line for the most part."

Wrecker's phone rang, and he shook his head when he saw who was calling. "I gotta take this. Check in tomorrow." He put the phone to his ear and headed down the hallway. Something was going on with him, but he wasn't talking.

Shit was going down at the clubhouse, and I wasn't around to keep up with it. I loved having Nikki all to myself, but I was missing things around here that I shouldn't be.

I was going to have to talk to Nikki and see where her head was. I know we had just started doing whatever the hell it was we were doing, but we were going to have a serious talk, and I had no idea how Nikki was going to take it.

*

Chapter 24

Nikki

"When he gets here, I'm telling him."

I grabbed Bos' arm and shook my head. "No, you are not. I will."

"You had over a week to tell him, and you never did."

"We were busy doing other things," I hissed.

Bos took off his apron and tossed it on the counter. "He's been done eating for over a half an hour, Nikki. Something ain't right."

"He's probably just lonely, Bos. I don't know why that makes him some creeper who wants to stuff me in his trunk."

Lights flashed across the diner, and we both turned to see Pipe step out of a truck. Bos dashed out from behind the grill, bolted in front of me, and swept out the door before I could even move.

I watched from the window as Bos flailed his arms around and looked like he was yelling at Pipe.

Pipe's eyes connected with mine through the window, and I knew Bos had told him.

Son of a gun.

Now he was going to be mad at me for not telling him about Richard. Even though I thought there wasn't anything to tell him. I had seen Richard three times since some creep took my picture, and Richard didn't act any different.

"Sugar," Pipe called.

I rolled my eyes and leaned against the counter. "You're a little early. Where is your bike?"

"I took care of the shit I needed to in Weston, and it's too cold for the bike. Truck until March."

"Hmm." I was going to miss the bike. "Well, are you hungry? I still have forty-five minutes left of my shift."

Pipe sat down at the counter. "I'll take whatever the special is today, and then you can sit next to me while I eat. From what Bos says, you have a story to tell me."

Bos walked back into the kitchen whistling under his breath, and I was half tempted to trip him to wipe that smug look off his face. "Special is pot roast with all the fixings."

"Sounds good to me, sugar."

I scribbled Pipe's order on my notepad and stuck it in the window for Bos. "You want coffee or something else to drink?"

"Coffee."

I set his cup down in front of me and looked over to where Richard was still sitting. "I need to go get him his change, and then I'll be back."

Pipe nodded. I felt him watching me the short walk over to Richard and glanced over my shoulder to see his eyes trained on me. If Richard tried anything except for paying for his dinner, he was going to have Pipe and Bos on his back.

"Can I get you another cup of coffee?" I asked.

Richard ducked his head and pushed the bill toward me. "No, all good."

"Okay, let me just get you some change and I—"

Richard put his hand on mine and shook his head. "No change," he muttered. "I was actually hoping that maybe we could figure out a day we could go on that date."

I snatched my hand back and looked over at Pipe who was staring directly at me. I shook my head, hoping he would understand I didn't need help, at least not yet. "Um, you know what? A guy I was seeing back in Weston showed up a few days ago, and we're back on for the moment."

Richard's face fell. "Oh, well, nevermind." He grabbed his coat, slid out from the booth, and almost ran out the door.

I shook my head and wondered if I should have told him what I did. I didn't want to lead him on, but I also didn't want to hurt his feelings.

"Nikki, get your ass over here right now."

I rolled my eyes and finished clearing Richard's table. "I'm still working. I don't have to listen to where you tell me to get my ass for another thirty-five minutes."

"Nikki, get your ass over to Pipe," Bos called from the window. He dinged the bell, and added, "Order up."

"It takes you ten minutes to make everyone else's meals, and suddenly Pipe wants dinner, and you have it done in two minutes." I grabbed the plates out of the window and set them in front of Pipe.

"Now, sit your ass down." Pipe pulled the plate to him and forked in a bite of the tender pot roast. "Shit, that's good."

"Best pot roast in a hundred mile radius," Bos bragged.

I rolled my eyes and grabbed a damp rag to wipe down the counter. "I think I'll just stand while you yell at me for no reason."

"The fact you have some creep asking you out is a reason."

"It's nothing, Pipe."

He took a sip of his coffee. "So the guy standing outside your house taking pictures is nothing too?"

"Which, by the way, is bullshit you didn't tell me about," Bos called. "After I drove you home and kept an eye on you the past month, you don't tell me when you have a stalker."

"I don't have a stalker," I insisted.

"The fact you aren't taking this seriously is shit, sugar. This Richard guy may be harmless, but we won't know that until I look into him. Bos said he's been known to get a bit stalkerish with women, so what happened to you sounds like some shit he would pull."

I tossed my rag on the counter. "Fine, check him out, but I think you two are wrong."

Pipe leveled his gaze at me and smirked. "If I'm wrong, then it won't hurt to check in on him."

"You're a bit of a dick, you know that?"

"And you're stubborn as hell. You know that?"

I curled my lip and shook my head. "You like it."

"That I do, sugar, that I do."

Pipe finished his dinner, shootin' the shit with Bos while I wiped down all the tables, and refilled any salt and pepper shakers that needed it.

"Ready to head home?" Pipe asked as I tossed my dirty apron in the hamper.

"If by home you mean my side of the duplex, then yeah. I'm not up for the roach motel tonight," I laughed. Pipe had been staying with me every night and just going over to his place to grab clean clothes every morning. I still couldn't believe my landlords had only remodeled half of the duplex and still rented out the hell hole side.

Pipe tossed a twenty on the counter, and I shoved it into the cash register. "You tip way too much," I mumbled.

He shrugged. "You gotta afford those leggings somehow, sugar. I'm just doing my part."

I rested my elbows on the counter and leaned in for a kiss. "Well, my legs thank you."

Pipe wrapped his hand around my neck and pulled me close. "I missed you, woman," he growled.

"You may have crossed my mind a couple of times," I replied coyly.

"You playing hard to get with me?" he growled.

I stood up straight and tossed my rag into the hamper. "I would try to, but we both know I end up giving in after about a week."

"Change of plans. We're not going out with your girl. I think I need to show you just how much I missed you today."

I rolled my eyes and pulled my phone from my pocket. "I guess that's doable." I sent off a quick message to Alice knowing she was going to be disappointed, but Pipe's plans sounded much more appealing than a few hours at The Bar.

Bos peeked his head out from the kitchen. "You two can head out. Lock the door on your way out. I gotta prep shit for tomorrow so I'll be another hour or so."

Pipe led me out the door and to the truck after I locked the door. I ran my hands up and down my arms, shivering. "Jesus, it is getting cold out here."

Pipe opened the door to the truck and helped me up. "Imagine being on the back of a bike in this."

I shook my head and shivered. "No thanks," I giggled. "I guess I'll just have to deal with riding next to you instead of behind you."

"Soon enough, sugar, we'll be back on the bike." He shut the door and rounded the front of the truck to the driver's side.

"I have to say I like your truck, though." It wasn't brand new, but you could tell it was well taken care of.

"Gets me where I need to go," he mumbled.

I yawned and rested my head against the window. "I do have to say, I can now fall asleep while you drive without worrying about the risk of road rash."

Pipe laughed and turned onto our street. "Yeah, I'd have to say that is a perk of having the truck."

"So, did you learn anything new in Weston today?"

Pipe pulled into the driveway and turned his head to look at me. "Some shit going on, but nothing we can't handle."

I scooted closer to him and rested my hand on his thigh. "Anything you wanna talk about?" I knew Pipe couldn't tell me certain things about the club, but I wanted him to know I was there if he ever did actually want to talk.

"Let's get in the house, and then we can talk."

I nodded, surprised he actually wanted to tell me what was going on.

Pipe grabbed my hand, tugged me across the seat, and helped me down.

"Did you see Karmen at all?"

Pipe unlocked the front door and held it open for me. One of the changes that had happened the past week. Now he had a key to my place and could come and go whenever he wanted. A huge step for me, but it felt right.

"Pretty sure she was working. I only saw the guys today. Cora was tucked away in her room, like normal."

I slipped my shoes off by the door and piled my hair up on top of my head with my hands. "Cut her some slack. She was dumped with you guys against her will. It can't be easy to have barely any say over your life."

Pipe chuckled. "Oh, she has some say. She talked Wrecker into letting her friend come stay with her at the clubhouse because she found herself some trouble."

"What?' I gasped. "What kind of trouble is she in?"

"I can't go into details, sugar, but it isn't anything we can't take care of. Maniac is going to have to deal with her for the most part. Dumbass volunteered to keep an eye on her before thinking it through." Pipe tossed his keys on the counter and bent over to unlace his boots. He toed them off and tucked them under the counter. "Pretty sure he's going to have his hands full with her."

I let go of my hair and moved to the fridge, trailing my fingers across Pipe's chest as I walked past him. "So tell me more about her. What's her name? You think she'll get along with Karmen and me?" Assuming whoever this chick was had to be like Cora, and while Cora got along well with Karmen and me, I wondered if she would.

"All I know is her name is Wren, and I assume she'll be at the clubhouse pretty quick. Wrecker didn't paint her troubles as the kind that she can sit around and wait to move in."

I grabbed the half-empty bottle of wine from the fridge and a bottle of beer for Pipe. "Wren, huh? That's a bit of a different name you don't hear often."

Pipe shrugged and reached up in the cabinet for a glass. "Didn't really think about it, sugar." He set the wine glass down on the counter and grabbed the bottle of wine from me. "You can put the beer back. I'm gonna hit the shower and then bed."

I stuck the beer back in the fridge and leaned against the counter as I watched him fill my glass. "Hmm, going to sleep pretty early tonight."

He handed me the glass. "Who said anything about sleeping?" He grabbed my empty hand and pulled me into the bathroom.

He turned on the water and pulled his shirt over his head. "You're either going to have to chug that or set it down because as soon as I get my clothes off, you're coming in the shower with me, glass in your hand or not."

I swirled my wine around in my glass. "I thought you said you wanted to talk?"

He shrugged and unbuttoned his pants. "There's always time for talking later."

I watched as he slowly dragged the zipper on his pants down and licked my lips.

"Ten seconds to chug and get your clothes off, sugar, or you're coming in the way you are."

"You're insane," I laughed. There was no way I was going in the shower in my uniform. "I think maybe you can shower by yourself, and I'll meet you in bed."

He shook his head and dropped his pants to the floor. "Five seconds," he warned.

A shiver ran through my body when his hands went to the waistband of his boxers and he pulled them down.

I set my wine glass down, deciding wine could wait when you had a badass alpha waiting for you.

*

Chapter 25

Nikki

"You wanna go to Weston with me tomorrow?"

I kicked off my shoes and started taking off my uniform. I had just worked a six-day stretch at work and was ready for two days off. "I don't care what we do tomorrow. It's finally my day off so as long as it doesn't involve going to the diner, I'm good." I shimmied my skirt down my hips and stepped out of it as I pulled my shirt over my head. "Wren is there, right?"

Pipe wrapped me up in his arms and pressed me against the door. "I really can't talk about shit when you're standing there in nothing but your sexy as hell panties."

I wrapped my arms around his neck and pressed a kiss to his cheek. "I would have thought you would have been sick of me by now."

"That shit ain't never going to happen, sugar. You can never get tired of an angel."

"I am far from an angel, Pipe," I laughed. "I'm pretty sure Bos was ready to fire me today after I dropped a full pot of coffee on the floor."

"Bos can kick rocks for all I care."

"Are you going to answer my question about Wren being at the clubhouse?" I asked.

"She got there two days ago. I haven't seen her yet. I talked to Wrecker today, and he said things are going fine. He mentioned something about a party tomorrow night, and I thought we could head down there for the night."

I tapped my chin, pretending to think about it. "Well, I guess we can go there. Alice did want us to come over and watch a movie with her tomorrow."

"Fuck that," Pipe scoffed. "If she wants to hang out with you, then she's going to have to come to the clubhouse with us."

"Really?" I asked, shocked.

"Yeah," he muttered. "Wrap your legs around me," he ordered. His hands went to my ass, he lifted me up, and my legs went around his waist.

"She can come with?"

"Sugar, didn't I just say that she could?" Pipe walked backwards a few steps, turned around, and headed toward the kitchen. I thought for sure he was headed to the bedroom, but instead, he pulled out a kitchen chair and sat down. "You're gonna ride me, right here."

"Oh, well this is new," I laughed.

"Lots of places to fuck you besides the bed, sugar. I thought we'd branch out tonight and try out the kitchen."

"Can't really argue with that, can I?"

"You sure fucking can't," he growled in my ear. He pressed searing kisses to my neck, traveling to my chin and down to my breasts. "How do you taste so good?"

"I'm pretty sure I smell like burnt toast and bacon right now, so I don't know exactly what you're tasting."

His body shook under me, and a chuckle rumbled against my skin. "Such a smartass."

I delved my fingers into his hair and pulled his head back. "So now I'm a smartass angel?"

"It works for you," he laughed.

"You know what else works for me?"

"What's that?"

"When you don't have any pants on. It's kind of hard to ride you through your jeans."

He grabbed me around the waist, my feet slid to the floor, and I stood up. "Pants come off when I see your tits."

"Has anyone ever told you you're a dirty man?"

He shook his head, folded his arms over his head, and leaned back. "Only you, sugar, but I know you like it."

"Sometimes," I mumbled. I wasn't exactly a fan of it when he picked me up two nights ago and proceeded to corner me in the kitchen while Bos was on his break. Pipe decided he needed to show me exactly why he liked my uniform so much. "Easy access," he had grunted as he pounded into me from behind and I had to bite my lip as I tried to hold back the moaning or moans. The man was a menace.

"Thinking about the diner?" he asked, with a smirk spreading across his lips.

"It's a good thing I like you because Alice gave me so much shit about that the next day. I can't believe you couldn't keep it in your pants until we got home."

"You weren't complaining then, sugar. If I recall correctly, I'm not the one who grabbed a washcloth and shoved it in their mouth to keep from screaming."

I reached around, unhooked my bra, and let it fall down my arms. "Well, then I guess it's payback tonight. I get to see what it takes to make you scream."

He pulled his shirt over his head and tossed it on the floor. "You're welcome to try, sugar. But I have a feeling you're the one who's going to be screaming while your pussy grips my dick like a vise."

"Promises, promises," I chided. Slipping my panties over my thighs and let them drop to the ground. "I'm gonna need your pants off. Now."

Pipe did as I asked, his pants and boxers gone in an instant. He sat back down, stroking his dick as his eyes roamed over my body. "You're fucking beautiful, Nikki."

"You're not so bad yourself, handsome." My hands slid over my body, cupping my breasts, and squeezing my hard nipples.

"Son of a bitch," he growled as I dropped to my knees and pushed his legs open.

I looked up, my eyes connecting with his. "Ready to scream?"

"I'm fucking ready for whatever you wanna give me, sugar."

I licked my lips and pushed his hand away. "Allow me," I whispered. My hand slid up and down the shaft of his rock hard cock while my other hand cupped his balls. My mouth watered as a drop of precum beaded on the tip of his dick, and I licked my lips.

"Better get that, sugar. Wouldn't want it to go to waste."

"So fucking dirty," I mumbled leaning forward. My tongue swiped the cum from his dick, and Pipe's thighs shook as a groan slipped from his lips.

"And you're so fucking hot. I want your mouth on my dick."

I shook my head and leaned back. "I'm calling the shots tonight, handsome."

My hand stroked his dick up and down, and his eyes were hooded, looking down at me. "As long as you don't stop touching me, I'm good with whatever you have planned for me."

"That's what I like to hear." My hand sped up, watching as his dick grew longer and harder. "God, you're dick is fucking amazing." Yeah, I said it, and I wasn't ashamed to admit it. I'm sure that went straight to the head on his shoulders, but I had never been in awe of a dick before.

"It's all because of you," he gasped. His breathing was labored, and he was gripping the edge of the chair while he watched my hand.

I stopped stroking his dick and ran my hands over his bare thighs. "It's all mine?" I asked as I leaned forward, my lips above his dick. "This is only for me?" I glanced up and found his bottom lip between his teeth.

"Yours," he panted.

His words hit my ears. Everything I wanted in one simple word.

My mouth opened. I bobbed up and down, his dick hitting the back of my throat, and I went back for more. I wanted every single piece of this man, his dick included.

He grabbed my hair, pulling it back, and held it up. "God damn, your fucking mouth is Heaven," he grunted.

I grabbed the base of his dick and stroked up, touching where my mouth couldn't reach. His fingers delved into my hair, gripped my head, and gently pulled my head up and down. "Tell me if it's too much, sugar." His hips thrust up, meeting my mouth as he pushed me down on his dick.

I laid my hands on his thighs and closed my eyes, enjoying the feel of him against my tongue. "Son of a bitch," he groaned when he hit the back of my throat, and I gagged a bit.

My nails sunk into his thigh as I relaxed my throat and took him deeper.

"Stop," he grunted. He pulled my head up, hooked his hands under my arms, and hauled me off the floor in one swipe.

"Stop?" I wiped my mouth with the back of my hand and looked down at Pipe. I was back to straddling his lap, and his dick was pointed up between us.

"I'm coming in that sweet cunt of yours."

I rested my hands on his shoulders and closed my eyes. "There's my dirty man."

"You fucking like it," he growled. He lifted me up again, lining up his dick with my pussy. "Open your eyes. I wanna watch you while I fuck you."

A smile spread across my lips, and I opened my eyes. "Pretty sure you can fuck me with my eyes closed."

He shook his head and lowered me onto his dick. "I wanna make sure you only see me and know whose dick is inside you."

I gasped and tossed my head back. "God," I moaned.

"Just call me Pipe, sugar." His hands gripped my ass, and he lifted me up, leaving just the tip inside me. "Or you can always call me Derek."

"Derek?" I tilted my head down and looked him in the eye. "Did you just tell me what your name is? In the middle of sex?"

He pressed a kiss to my lips. "Figured it was a good time," he mumbled against me.

"Does this mean I call you Derek now?"

He shook his head. "No. Or you can, but not when anyone else is around."

"Hmm, I guess I accept that."

He lifted me up again and hammered into me. "Good," he grunted.

"Oh, my God," I moaned. I buried my face in his neck and bit down on his shoulder.

"Son of a bitch, Nikki."

I pressed kisses up his neck, and my gaze fell on the window. "What th—" A scream ripped from my lips, and I pushed off, falling flat on my ass. "Th-the-the window!"

Pipe jumped up and turned around just in time to see a man running down the driveway. "What the fuck!" he yelled. He grabbed his pants off the floor, hopping into them as he walked into the kitchen and reached up in the cabinet above the fridge.

"What are you—" My question was answered before I even got the words out.

Pipe pulled down a gun, slammed the cabinet shut, and pointed at me. "Lock the door, call nine-one-one, and get dressed. Don't move." He was out the door in only a pair of jeans and a gun in his hands, and he ran down the driveway in the same direction the man had run.

I scrambled off the floor, locked the door behind him, and pulled my phone out of my purse that I had dropped on the floor.

My hands shook as I brought up the keypad on my phone and punched in nine-one-one.

"Nine-one-one, what is your emergency?"

"Um, my boyfriend is chasing a man down the street who was watching us…"

"Watching you what, ma'am?" The dull voice on the other end asked.

"Uh, we were having sex, and some guy was watching us."

"Can I get your address, please? I'll get a squad dispatched to your house."

I rattled off my address and hung up the phone after the dispatcher told me the police should be here within five minutes. I crept toward the window and looked out to see if Pipe was nearby.

My eye caught my reflection in the mirror, and I remembered the last thing Pipe had told me to do.

Get dressed.

*

Chapter 26

Pipe

"Okay, I think we have everything we need. We'll be in touch if we find anything or if we have any other questions."

Pipe nodded to the police officer who looked to be no older than twenty. "We'd appreciate that."

By the time the police had arrived, Pipe was walking through the door and stashed the gun he had grabbed before above the fridge.

"I'd advise keeping your curtains closed until we find whoever is doing this." The officer tipped his hat at me and walked out the door.

Pipe shut the door behind him and leaned against it. "Now this creep is really starting to piss me off."

This creep was starting to scare me, and well, creep me out. "I can't believe I didn't notice him standing there." I ran my fingers through my hair and plopped down on the couch. I had managed to put on a pair of leggings and a shirt before Pipe had gotten back to the house and the cop showed up. My skin was crawling, and I just felt dirty. I rubbed my arms and hung my head. "I just can't," I whispered.

I listened as I heard Pipe close the curtains and lock the front door. "Get up, sugar. You and I are going to shower and then we're going to bed."

I looked up and shook my head. "Please, I really don—"

"Stop. I'm not talking sex. I'm talking we shower, and then we try to sleep."

"I don't think I can sleep right now." My head was a complete mess. I was ten times more terrified than the last time this had happened. Whoever this guy was had watched me at my most intimate moment with Pipe. Being with Pipe was meant for only me and him.

"Whatever you want. We can watch a movie, play a game, read a book. Whatever you want."

I nodded and stood. "Okay." I wasn't sure how good of company I was going to be, but Pipe didn't seem to really care. "Are you sure the curtains are closed enough?"

Pipe grabbed my hand and pulled me down the hallway as I wearily looked over my shoulder at the window. "They're closed, sugar. Try not to worry about it."

I sighed and leaned against the sink. Pipe turned on the water and pulled the shower curtain shut. "Clothes off." He was still wearing only his pants and tugged them down his legs.

"I just feel off," I muttered. I looked around and rubbed my hands together. I knew no one was watching us now, but I couldn't shake the feeling someone was.

"Hey," Pipe called. He grabbed my hand and wrapped me up in his arms.

I shivered and buried my head in his chest. "I'm sorry," I mumbled.

"There isn't anything to be sorry for, sugar. I'm here. Nothing is going to happen to you."

"I don't know why this is happening. What did I do?"

"Hey, hey." His hand caressed my cheek and gently tilted my head back to look up at him. "You didn't do anything wrong. I don't know why this guy is doing this, but we'll get it figured out. Between me and the police, this guy is more than caught."

"I don't want you to go looking for him. What if when you chased after him tonight, he hurt you? I couldn't have lived with myself knowing you got hurt because of me."

He shook his head and pressed a kiss to my forehead. "I'm telling you right now, sugar, this guy is not going to hurt you or me. He's a coward who stands in the shadows. He doesn't stand a chance."

"Okay," I whispered. I trusted Pipe would keep me safe, but I was still worried he was going to get hurt doing it. "We should probably hop in the shower." The steam was billowing over the top of the curtain and fogging up the mirror.

Pipe helped me strip down, taking extra care of me. His hands ran over my body, and he pressed a kiss to my collarbone. "You're mine, Nikki, and I always take care of what's mine."

I face-planted into his chest and sighed. "Thank you."

I loved this man.

He was my rock when I was scared.

My shield when I needed protecting.

My soft place to land when I'd had a hard day.

He was mine, and I was the luckiest damn woman in the world.

*

Chapter 27

Pipe

"Sugar, wake up." I gently shook Nikki's shoulder, and she burrowed into my side.

"No, I'm too tired to move."

"All you need to do is get in my room, and you can go back to sleep."

Her head lifted, and she looked out the windshield. "We're here?"

"Yeah. You fell asleep as soon as we hit the highway."

She looked up at me and yawned. "I'm sorry. I didn't think I could sleep, but apparently, I was wrong."

I brushed her hair back from her face. "I think it had something to do with the fact we weren't in Kales Corners anymore."

After we had showered last night, we both fell into bed, but Nikki never really slept. She would doze off for about half an hour then wake up frantic, flailing her arms and screaming. I would finally get her settled only for her to wake up again. I was beyond exhausted and had thought about not going to Weston, but I figured it would be good for her to get out Kales Corners.

Alice was asleep in the backseat and was snoring away.

Nikki peaked over the seat and laughed. "I think she wore herself out worrying about coming here. She was pretty shocked when I called her this morning and invited her to come with us."

Excited was an understatement. I had been brewing a pot of coffee when I heard Alice scream through the phone. Nikki had been sitting in the living room and had moved the phone from her ear because she had screamed so loud.

Alice had stayed awake maybe ten minutes longer than Nikki, and then she was out like a light.

"Are you talking about me?" Alice asked sleepily from the back.

"You are the only one who freaked out about coming here," Nikki laughed.

Alice sat up and stuck her head into the front. "How do I look? Think I can catch myself a biker?"

Nikki squinted, and I tried not to laugh. Her hair was plastered to the side of her head, and she had a huge red line on her face from where she had fallen asleep on the zipper of her coat. "Um, you might want to fluff up your hair a bit." Nikki adjusted the rearview mirror and pointed it at Alice.

"Jumpin' Jehoshaphat! What did you do to me?" She licked her hand and ran it down the side of her hair.

"Me?" I asked. "I didn't do shit, woman."

She shook her head and rubbed a hand down her face. "What happened to my face?" she screeched.

"It's really not that bad, Alice. Just run your fingers through your hair, and the line on your face will be gone in no time," Nikki reassured her.

I opened my door, pulling Nikki out behind me. "Get the lead out, woman. None of the guys will care what you look like."

Nikki slapped me on the chest, and Alice yelled, "You're an asshole."

Well, that wasn't necessary. "What'd I do?" I asked Nikki.

"You can't tell her no one will care what she looks like," she hissed.

"I didn't mean it, well, meanly. I just meant she looks fine the way she is." She did look fine. Maybe a little sleepy, but she was fine.

"Nikki!" Karmen barreled down on us and wrapped Nikki up into a huge hug. "I can't believe that you're actually here. There's too much to tell you over the phone. You can stay at my house, and we can catch up."

"Hell no." That was not fucking happening. There was no way in hell Nikki was going to spend the night away from me. I felt much safer being back in Weston, but I was still worried about the psycho watching her. "She's in my room."

Karmen scoffed and waved her hand at me. "No. You've had her for two weeks. It's my turn with her."

Nikki wearily looked at Karmen and shook her head. "I, uh, I think I'd rather stay with Pipe. No offense, but I just feel safer with him."

"Safer?" Karmen repeated. "What the hell does that mean? If he is going to keep you from falling out of bed because that's about the only thing I think he needs to keep you safe from."

Nikki looked at me and bit her lip. "Um, well…"

"What the hell is going on?" Karmen demanded.

I opened Alice's door. "Get out, woman. I'm not going to repeat myself, so you need to hear what's going on too."

"Going on? You mean other than my shit-tastic hair?" I grabbed her arm and pulled her out of the truck. "Yes, there are more important things going on other than your hair."

"Yo, you're back," Nickel called.

Karmen turned around and put her hands on her hips. "Something is going on. Do you know what's going on?" she asked Nickel.

Nickel looked at me, and I shook my head. He didn't know what was going on, but he got the clue I didn't want to discuss it in the parking lot.

"I don't know what's going on, baby girl, but I think we should let them get into the clubhouse, and then we can talk."

Karmen stomped her foot, but she let Nickel grab her hand and pull her into the clubhouse.

"Is this about Richard?" Alice asked. She grabbed her bag from the truck and hitched it over her shoulder.

"It might be."

"Lord help us." Alice hooked her arm through Nikki's and nodded her head at me. "Well, lead the way, badass."

I quirked my eyebrow and looked at Nikki. A smile spread across her lips, and she nodded at the clubhouse. "Well, you heard her, badass, lead the way," she giggled.

It was good to see Nikki laugh, but I knew she was still worried about whoever was watching her. "Grab Wrecker," I hollered to Nickel.

He lifted his hand and disappeared into the clubhouse.

"This is so cool," Alice whispered behind me. "Who's Wrecker?"

"Um, big bearded, burly guy who's the president," Nikki informed her.

"What a wicked name. So much better than Pipe."

I looked over my shoulder and smirked. "You can say that until you find out the reason they call me Pipe."

Alice's jaw dropped, and Nikki pointed her finger at me. "I'm gonna need to hear that story."

"Me too," Alice chirped. "You're like my personal biker whisperer for any questions I'll have this weekend."

"Um, I don't know what questions you'll have, but whatever, darlin'."

"Is it bad I swoon a little bit when he calls me that? It's purely because no one ever calls me that," she assured Nikki. "Not that I have the hots for your personal biker."

"Is that kind of like a personal shopper?" Nikki giggled. "And what questions are you going to have that I won't be able to answer?"

I opened the door and motioned for the girls to go ahead of me.

"Wrecker said to meet him in church." Nickel had his arm over Karmen's shoulder and disappeared down the hallway.

"Oh you know," Alice mumbled. "Can I talk to everyone? Do I have to avoid eye contact?"

Nikki looked at me, her eyes bugged out. "Avoid eye contact?" she asked me.

I shook my head. "We're not that kind of club, Alice. Just show us respect, and we'll show you respect back."

She nodded and headed in the direction Nikki and Karmen had. "Cool. See, it's good I asked. Otherwise, they would have thought I was shady."

I chuckled under my breath, and Nikki tried not to smile. "Yup, good thing you asked," she smirked.

The door to church was open, and Nickel was standing at the head of the table, talking to Wrecker.

"Wow," Alice gasped under her breath. "Hello, burly bearded man."

"Wrecker," I called. "You know Nikki. This is her friend Alice from Kales Corners."

Alice walked up to him, stuck her hand out to shake his, and I kid you not, fucking curtsied. "Mr. President," she mumbled.

Wrecker took her hand, watching her bowed head, and looked between Nickel and me. "Uh, no need to cursty, darlin'," he mumbled.

She lifted her head and looked Wrecker directly in the eye. "It's so great to be allowed in your club."

"Sweet Jesus, Alice," Karmen laughed. "He's the president of the Weston chapter, not the President of the United States."

Alice curtsied again and stepped back from Wrecker. "Sorry, your highness."

Nickel smothered his laugh with the back of his hand and looked at Nikki. "Is this shit for real?"

Nikki shrugged. "Maybe we shouldn't have brushed off the fact she had questions," she mumbled, looking up at me.

"Yeah, you might be right, sugar."

Alice looked around the table. "Can I sit anywhere?"

Alice was in her own little world and had no idea that we were talking about her.

"Uh, you can sit anywhere. This isn't an official meeting or anything," Wrecker explained.

Of course, Alice sat in the chair I normally did. She pulled her chair in and rested her hands on the table. "I'm pretty sure I'm gonna wet my pants if anything else cool happens."

Wrecker, Nickel, and I busted out laughing, and the girls all giggled.

Wrecker sat down at the head of the table, while Nickel took his normal spot next to him and sat Karmen next to him.

Nikki sat down next to Alice, and I sat down in the chair meant for just a regular member. It had been a long time since I had sat this far down at the table. "Some shit has been going down in Kales Corners, and I thought I should let you know before something else happens."

"Trouble always seems to follow you girls," Wrecker muttered.

"Hey," Karmen protested. "My trouble found me, and I'm sure the same goes for Nikki."

Wrecker waved his hand at her. "Details, darlin'."

Wrecker could definitely be a bit of a dick when he wanted to be.

Nickel patted Karmen's leg and whispered in her ear. She crossed her arms over her chest but didn't try to argue with Wrecker.

Wrecker turned to me and nodded his head. "Tell me what's going on."

"Does anyone else feel like he's the godfather?" Alice whispered loudly to Nikki.

Jesus, this was a complete shit show. Thankfully, the rest of the club wasn't here. Everyone would have been rolling with laughter, and I never would have been able to talk. I cleared my throat and leveled a glare on Alice for her to shut her mouth.

She made a motion to zipper her lips, and turned to Wrecker, holding out what I assumed was the imaginary key she used to lock her lips up.

"Sweet Jesus." He held out his hand, and she dropped the fake key in it. He nodded at Alice and pretended to tuck the key into his pocket. To Alice, I'm sure she thought he was okay, but from the way his jaw ticked, and look he gave me, I knew I was going to get hell for this.

Wrecker was going to beat the shit out of me after this meeting was over.

I cleared my throat and hoped to God Alice wouldn't get up to any more crazy antics.

"He gets the key because he's the president," she whispered to Nikki.

Nikki nodded. "Good idea," she whispered.

I needed to get this over with and get Alice far, far away from Wrecker. I could tell he was holding his tongue, and that never lasted long.

"About a couple of weeks ago, Nikki noticed someone standing outside of her house taking pictures. She came over to my place as soon as she saw it, but I was too late to catch whoever it was. Nothing happened after that except for last night the guy was back, and he was watching Nikki and me."

Karmen gasped and flattened her hands on the table. "Someone was watching you? Oh, my God. Who is it?"

"We're still trying to figure that out. I almost caught him last night, but I had to grab my pants and gun before I could go after him."

Alice turned to Nikki. "He had to put his pants on?" she asked with her eyebrow raised. "Y'all were getting it on, weren't you?"

Nikki blushed and ducked her head.

"Duh, of course, they were, Alice," Karmen laughed.

Wrecker snickered but knew not to give me shit about it in front of Nikki.

"We called the police, but I don't have much faith in them finding this guy since the most they deal with in that town is the occasional speeder or jaywalker."

Wrecker leaned forward and rested his forearms on the table. "You have any idea of who this might be?"

"Nikki caught the eye of one of her customers at work, and I think it's him. Her boss told me that this wouldn't be the first time this guy took his infatuation to a new level."

"So why haven't you grabbed the guy and asked him what the hell he's doing?"

"Because I can't believe that it's him," Nikki piped up. "I can't believe that this man who can barely get a full sentence out when talking to me is capable of doing this."

Wrecker sat back in his chair. "It sounds exactly what someone like that would do. He's standing outside of your window watching you and your man together. He's a fucking coward."

Nikki stared down at the table. "I guess you're right, but I just don't understand why he would do this."

"Because he doesn't have balls, darlin'," Nickel stated.

She sighed and slumped her shoulders. "Fine. We assume it's Richard. Now, what do we do? This guy isn't all there upstairs mentally. I don't want him to get hurt."

Wrecker rolled his eyes. "So you just wanna let him keep watching you get your rocks off every night because there ain't no birdie in his cuckoo clock?"

"Well, no. I just mean I don't want you guys showing up to his house and breaking his kneecaps."

"Darlin', we don't break kneecaps. They can still talk after that," Nickel smirked.

Karmen elbowed him in the side. "Not helping," she hissed.

Nickel shrugged and leaned back in his chair. "So what do you want us to do since we're not allowed to hurt poor Richard?"

"Can't we just get him to confess, and then turn him over to the police?" Alice suggested. "I know Richard too, and he isn't playing with a full deck of cards. He's done this kind of thing before, but never like he's doing to Nikki."

"Fine. I'm gonna send Slayer and Brinks up there. See what they can dig up, and try to talk some sense into this guy. I'm sure it won't take much for them to get this guy to talk about what he's doing." Wrecker looked at Nikki. "That fine with you?"

"I'm sorry. I don't mean to be such a Sally about this. I guess bustin' kneecaps isn't my style."

I put my arm around her shoulders and pulled her close. "You're fine, sugar. This'll give Slayer and Brinks a chance to work on their people skills, right Wrecker?"

"If anything, with those two talking to this guy, they'll probably just scare him away. I doubt anyone has ever tried to talk to this guy before." He pointed his finger at Nickel. "Make sure your woman doesn't get any ideas and try to take care of this guy herself."

Karmen gasped. "Hey, I'm sitting right here."

"I'll talk to Slayer and Brinks. When are you heading back up?" Wrecker asked.

"We're here for the weekend."

Wrecker stood up and grabbed his sunglasses off the table. "I'll have them head up there tonight. You good with them staying at your place?"

I pulled my keys out of my pocket, slipped the duplex key off, tossing it to Wrecker. "It's all theirs."

"That. Was. Awesome," Alice squealed when Wrecker walked out of the room. "That man is smokin' hot. Do you think if I asked nicely he would let me pet his beard?"

Nikki turned to Alice. "Maybe if you curtsy first."

Karmen threw her head back, laughing her ass off, and I couldn't help but chuckle.

"Next time, try kissing his knuckles. That might loosen him up a bit," Nickel added.

"Hey," Alice protested. "How was I supposed to know how to act around him? The man is intimidating as hell."

"He's intimidating, Alice, not the king of England," I said over the top of Nikki's head.

She stuck her tongue out at me and crossed her arms over her chest. "You're an ass. Both of you." She glared at me and turned to Nickel. "I'm surprised your super sweet girlfriend's put up with your shit."

Nickel shrugged and stood up. "What can I say? I've got an amazing personality and huge dick."

Karmen gasped, choking on her own spit. "Jesus Christ, man. You did not just say that," she hissed.

Nikki looked up at me. "That's the same reasons you have."

I shrugged. "At least you recognize my stellar qualities."

"Stellar indeed," she said, winking at me.

Alice pushed back from the table and stood up. "Okay, now that we established you both have big dicks, you think I can get a tour of the clubhouse?"

"Yeah," I laughed. "I'll show you where you'll be staying."

"I wanna meet Wren," Nikki piped up. "Is she with Cora?"

Karmen shot up. "Dude, she is super cool. You're going to love her."

"We'll swing by her room on the tour of the clubhouse. She normally hangs out in Cora's room all day," Nickel suggested.

I grabbed Nikki's hand and pulled her up. "Come on, sugar."

She stood up and rested her hand on my shoulder. "Thank you," she whispered.

I knew it had killed Wrecker to agree to not hurt Richard, but I knew that was what Nikki wanted. I was down with kicking the guy's ass just like Nickel, but I didn't want to upset Nikki. "We try it your way first, sugar. If that doesn't work, then it's my way."

She rolled her eyes but agreed. "Fine. But I don't want to know anything if we do it your way."

"That's doable, sugar."

"Hello," Alice called. "Can I get a tour of the badass clubhouse filled with badasses?"

I pressed a kiss to Nikki's forehead and smiled. "Your friend is a nutjob."

Nikki laughed and looked up at me. "She totally is."

At least we agreed on that.

*

Chapter 28

Nikki

"I love this kid, but honestly, I can't wait 'til I can have a drink."

"At least Nickel isn't drinking either," I pointed out.

We were sitting at a table by the pool table, watching Pipe and Nickel play. "Yeah, that is nice of him. Although I did catch him sneaking a beer the other night."

I laughed and took a sip of my wine. "You yell at him?"

"Nah, he deserves it. He's been doing a lot of shit for the club lately, and I know he's stressed out."

"You mean with Wren?" Who, by the way, we had yet to meet. When we had given Alice her tour of the clubhouse, Cora said she had a headache and had gone to lie down. She had promised that she would be out for the party tonight.

"No. I think there is other stuff going on. From what Nickel said, Wren is Maniac's problem."

That was news to me. Although I knew I wouldn't always know what was going on with the club, I had hoped Pipe would talk to me if he needed to. "Have you seen Alice?"

Karmen laughed. "I heard she asked Wrecker to take her for a ride on his bike."

"Shut up," I gasped. "I think she might be barking up the wrong tree with Wrecker."

Karmen nodded. "That you are right, sister. I think she's more infatuated with the fact he's the president."

I shrugged and peeled the label off my beer. "Or, you know, they could be perfect for one another. I mean, did you really expect me and Pipe to hook up?"

"Well, I knew you wanted a biker of your own, but no, I never thought it would actually happen. I mean, come on, did you think Nickel and I would hook up and he would get me pregnant?" she laughed. "Anything is possible, Nikki."

"What's possible?" Nickel asked as he picked up his beer from the table.

"Alice and Wrecker hooking up."

Nickel choked on his beer. "Yeah, that shit isn't happening."

"Why not?" I demanded. Alice was a bit cuckoo, but there wasn't anything wrong with her.

"Because we're pretty sure Wrecker has a chick on the side we don't know."

"What?" Karmen gasped. "And you're just now telling me this? Who is it?" she demanded. "We could add another chick to our Girl Gang."

"Girl gang?" Pipe asked. He leaned down and pressed a kiss to the side of my head. "You good, sugar?" he asked quietly.

I looked up at him and nodded. "Totally good. We were just talking about Wrecker and Alice hooking up, and then Karmen mentioned a Girl Gang. Not really sure where she was headed with that one."

"We're never really sure where Karmen is headed with anything," he snickered.

"It's a good thing I'm pregnant and sober. Otherwise, I would totally kick your butt." She looked Pipe up and down and took a sip of her soda. "Or have Nickel kick your butt."

"Well, I'm glad to know my butt is safe tonight."

I slapped him on the chest and shook my head. "Stop messing with her," I laughed.

"Like shooting fish in a barrel, sugar."

"Anywho," Karmen said, ignoring Pipe. "I was talking about our Girl Gang. It's me, Nikki, Cora, and Alice right now. It would be super cool to add Wren to it."

"Speaking of Wren," Nickel said, pointing over my shoulder. "There's your latest recruit right now."

I turned around and saw Cora walking toward our table with a short, curvy brunette. "Wow, she's super pretty." Her long brown hair had blonde highlights in it, giving it that sun-kissed look, and her skin was flawless. You know how guys say they like a woman with curves on her in all the right places? Well, Wren fit that description perfectly. She was wearing a pair of tight jeans that hugged her hips and butt, giving her the perfect silhouette. The dark plum shirt she wore looked amazing against her tanned skin, and well, she just looked hot.

Pipe pulled out the chair next to me and leaned close. "Poor Maniac thought the same thing until he had to watch her twenty-four seven. Pretty sure the poor guy is going to lose his shit before her troubles are over."

"Hey," Cora called. "This is Wren."

Wren gave a small wave and looked down at the floor.

Hmm, now this was interesting. I thought for sure she was going to be talkative, but instead, she looked like she wanted to be anywhere but here.

I stood up and held out my hand. "I'm Nikki, it's nice to meet you."

She gently shook my hand and gave me a small smile.

It was crazy how she and Cora were best friends. Where Cora was loud, outspoken, and boisterous, Wren was shy, quiet, and rather introverted.

"This is Pipe," I said, looking down at him.

He gave Wren a two finger salute. "Nice to meet you."

She blushed and nodded her head. "It's nice to meet you."

"Why don't you guys have a seat? Pipe and Nickel were just taking a break from playing pool, but I think they were just about to start another game. You guys can play with Maniac."

I looked past Wren and Cora and saw Maniac leaning against the pool table with his arms crossed over his chest. He did not look happy at all.

"We'll keep an eye on Wren," Karmen called to him. "You run along and play with the boys."

It cracked me up when Karmen talked to these guys like they were a bunch of twelve-year-olds. Where Alice acted like these guys were all gods, Karmen treated them all like her little brothers.

Pipe pressed a kiss to my forehead and mumbled a warning to behave.

Cora sat down in the chair Pipe had left, and Wren scooted into one between Karmen and Cora.

Karmen had a huge smile on her lips, and she rubbed her belly. "This is going to be amazing."

Cora leaned into me. "What the hell is she talking about?"

"I'm really as lost as you are. She was talking about a Girl Gang before you came over. I can only imagine what she's talking about," I whispered.

Cora sat back and looked at Karmen. "You're crazy."

"So subtle," I mumbled.

"Subtle goes over the head of crazy."

"I'm going to accept your crazy." Karmen turned to Wren. "Crazy is fun. And besides, every crazy thing I do, I can blame on the baby. He may keep me from drinking, but the kid is a pretty good alibi for whatever I want."

Wren laughed and looked down at Karmen's belly. "I could see that working. Everyone wants Burger King at one o'clock in the morning now and then, so this way you can say you have no control over it because the baby wants it. Totally going to have to remember that if I ever have a kid."

"Stick with me, and I'll tell you all my secrets."

I laughed and finished my beer. "If by secrets you mean crazy, then yeah, she can totally show you all of that."

Karmen shook her finger at me. "Hey, you're supposed to be on my side with this."

I held up my hands. "I'm totally on your crazy train."

"I feel this Girl Gang thing is very prisonesque. Do we have to wear stripes? I'm telling you right now, if it involves stripes, I'm out." Cora held up her hands. "This body is not made for stripes of any kind."

Karmen rolled her eyes. "Now who is the crazy one thinking we're going to have uniforms. Although, we could totally get shirts made up." Karmen tapped her chin and pulled out her phone. "I'm gonna google the price of getting custom shirts made."

"And she's back to being the crazy one," I laughed.

"I don't really understand what this Girl Gang is," Wren replied.

"Basically we're all friends who have each other's back. Like if Pipe is riding Nikki hard, we can back her up."

"Uh, am I the only who took that the completely wrong way?" Cora laughed.

"Yeah, if Pipe is riding me hard, then I really don't think I need your guy's backup or anything," I giggled.

"Oh Jesus," Karmen sighed. "You all know what I meant. I think your dry spell is affecting your brain, Cora."

Cora shrugged. "I really can't argue against that, because I believe you are completely correct."

"I think I'm going to be joining you on that dry spell so you won't be alone," Wren laughed.

"Well, y'all can have the Dry Spell Gang then because I can tell you right now that is one club Nikki and I will not be joining," Karmen said smugly.

Pipe came over to grab his beer in time to hear Karmen.

"What the hell are you guys talking about?" he demanded.

Karmen flicked her hand at him. "Don't worry. The Dry Spell Gang is a division of the Girl Gang. Nikki isn't joining that division."

Pipe tilted his head. "I'm not really sure what you just said, but it sounds like I'm still getting laid, right?"

Cora and Wren busted out laughing, and I just looked up at the man who managed to make me fall in love with him.

"You're still good, handsome."

He nodded. "All right, then carry on, ladies." He threw a wink at me and moved back over to the pool table.

Cora demanded to know exactly what Karmen meant by Girl Gang but I tuned them out and just watched Pipe as he lined up shots and talked with Nickel and Maniac.

I was one lucky woman to have that man in my bed every night.

The Dry Spell Gang was one I had no intention of joining, especially tonight.

*

Chapter 29

Pipe

"Get there, Nikki."

Her moan surrounded me as her fingers stroked her clit. I powered into her from behind, with her face smashed into the pillow and her ass in the air.

"Pipe, please," she pleaded.

I gritted my teeth, and I felt her pussy grip my cock as I thrust into her. "Yes, yes," I growled.

A scream ripped from her lips, and she reared back into me, burying my cock deep into her cunt.

I thrust hard, slamming into her while her pussy milked my cock. My cum filled her, and I gave one last thrust. "Fuck me," I muttered.

"I just did," she gasped.

I collapsed next to her and gathered her in my arms. "How the fuck do you always make it better than the last?"

"Pretty sure that is a group effort between the two of us," she giggled.

I shook my head and pressed a kiss to her temple. "Nah, I know it has everything to do with you."

She sighed and relaxed into my arms. "Whatever you say, handsome."

I reached down and grabbed the blanket that had been kicked to the foot of the bed. "Did you have a good night, sugar?" I pulled the blanket over us and laid my head down on my pillow.

"It was fun. I really like Wren."

"She seems cool enough." I hadn't spent much time with her, but I could see Nikki had liked her. Most of the night, I had listened to Maniac bitch and moan about having to watch her when all she did was hang out in Cora's room or her own. He didn't know why she needed to be watched twenty-four seven when she wasn't doing anything.

"Do you think we should have waited for Alice to get back before coming to bed?" she asked sleepily.

"Alice is a big girl, and Wrecker is one of the guys you can trust with her."

She nodded and closed her eyes. "I think I'm going to take a nap," she mumbled.

"Sleep, sugar," I whispered into her hair.

She snuggled closer to me and rested her head on my shoulder. "I don't know if it's the alcohol talking or the fact I'm exhausted, but I'm totally falling in love with you, Pipe."

"Same here, sugar," I whispered

A smile spread across her lips, and her breathing evened out as she fell asleep.

It had nothing to do with the booze, and I was wide awake.

I loved Nikki.

*

Nikki

Dear God, I thought sleepily.

I can't believe I just told him that.

I was a complete fool, but there was no taking it back right now.

Pipe Marks was making me fall in love with him, and I never wanted it to stop.

*

Chapter 30

Nikki

"I need more hot sauce."

I handed the hot sauce to Karmen and watched her empty a quarter of the bottle onto her eggs. "I'm not sure if that's as bad as ketchup on your eggs, or worse."

Karmen set down the hot sauce, picked up her fork, and dug into her hot sauce-laden eggs. "It's delicious," she said around a mouthful.

"Do you get heartburn?" Wren asked her.

"Sometimes."

"I'm not surprised," she laughed. "I'm sure your baby is going to have a full head of hair when he finally pops out."

"As long as he looks like Nickel, I don't care."

"Then he's going to need hair." I laughed.

"Can you imagine Nickel with a shaved head?" Cora asked.

"He'd look like Mr. Clean if he's bald."

Karmen shook her head and shoveled more food into her mouth. "He better have hair," she mumbled.

Alice shuffled into the small kitchen of the clubhouse and headed straight for the coffeemaker.

"Well, good morning, sunshine," Cora called. "I see you had such an amazing night you didn't even have time to change into your cow onesie."

Alice grabbed a coffee cup down from the cabinet and filled it full. "I'm not made for this club life. I just did one night of partying, and I'm ready to sleep for ten days."

Cora patted the chair next to her. "Come tell momma all about it."

Alice squinted at her. "I'm pretty sure I'm the same age, or possibly older than you."

"Really?" Cora turned to me. "How old do I look?"

Uh, I felt like this was a loaded question. If I guessed too high, then I would insult her, and if I went too low, I would look like I was trying to suck up. "I'm gonna have to say twenty-seven. Possibly twenty-eight, but that's as high as I'm going."

A grin spread across her lips, and she looked back at Alice. "I'm twenty-eight."

"I'm thirty-one. Me calling you momma creeps me out more than you know." Alice shuffled over to the chair by Cora and looked down at her. "The cow onesie makes me look younger, doesn't it?"

Cora blinked slowly. "I've tried to block that from my memory. Please don't bring it up again."

Alice pulled out the chair and plopped down. "No need to bring it up, I'll just put it on tonight, and you can see it again in all its glory."

"Um, did I miss something?" Wren asked.

I held up my hand. "It's best you don't know about Alice's collection of animal onesies."

Karmen's jaw dropped. "She has more than one?"

A huge smile spread across Alice's face. "I think you need to come to Kales Corners and see for yourself."

"What other animals could there possibly be?" Karmen had just opened a can of worms I was not looking forward to.

Alice took a long sip from her coffee and set it on the table. "Well, it all started with my cow one. He's my favorite." Alice prattled on about different animal onesies, but my attention was on Pipe and Maniac who were headed to the kitchen.

I bit my lip and took in everything that was Pipe. Long, powerful legs. Strong muscular arms covered with tattoos. Broad shoulders capable of carrying a heavy load. Dark, thick wavy hair.

Mine.

All mine.

He caught me staring, and a smirk spread across his lips. He reached into his pocket and stuck a cigarette in his mouth.

Goddamn, he was sexy as hell when he did that. I knew all the things he could do with his mouth, and my envy of a cigarette was ridiculous.

"Mornin', sugar," he mumbled as he leaned down and pressed a kiss to my neck.

Commence full-on goosebumps. Was I ever going to get used to this man touching me?

"Any food left?" Maniac asked. He walked to the stove and looked down at the empty pan of eggs and the pathetic one piece of bacon that was left. "Jesus, you would think a football team ate, not four chicks," he scoffed.

I looked up at Pipe. "I planned on making more eggs when you guys woke up. I didn't think you would want cold eggs."

"Is that the story you're sticking with, sugar?" he smirked.

I had made a shit ton of eggs, but I hadn't anticipated Karmen's raging appetite. "It is," I laughed.

Pipe stepped back and let me stand up, but not before he moved in and wrapped his arms around me.

I grabbed the cigarette out of his mouth. "There are much better things you can be doing with your mouth instead of smoking."

He brushed my hair off my neck and pressed a kiss next to my ear. "You mean that thing I did to you last night? Because I can totally clear this table and show everyone exactly what you mean." His tongue grazed my skin and pressed a trail of kisses down my neck.

"Holy shit," Cora gasped. "Do y'all see this? I'm pretty sure we have a front row seat to one of those soft porns where they keep their clothes on, but it's still sexy as fuck."

I buried my head in Pipe's chest and tried to fight back the embarrassment that was creeping up my face. The man sure knew how to make me forget where I was and see only him.

"Hand me your phone, Maniac. I could totally use this later with B.O.B."

Oh Jesus. I didn't need to know that Cora was going to think of Pipe and me when she used her toy.

"Who the fuck is Bob?" Maniac asked.

I pulled out of Pipe's arms and moved to the stove. I tossed his cigarette on the counter and tried to get my wits about me. I kept my head down and grabbed a bowl to crack the eggs into.

"It's not Bob, it's B.O.B.," Karmen explained not so clearly. "Battery operated boyfriend."

"Oh Jesus," Maniac cried. "I did not need that damn visual."

I looked over my shoulder and watched Cora cackle while she high-fived Karmen. "You know what it's about, girlfriend." Cora elbowed Wren, but she just sat there with her head down.

Before Pipe and Maniac had come in the room, she seemed to have come out of her shell a bit and was laughing and joking with us. Now the girl who looked like she wanted to be anywhere but here was back.

"Um, I think I'm going to head to my room," she mumbled. She grabbed her plate off the counter and dumped it in the sink next to me.

"Hey," I replied, gently grabbing her arm. She froze under my touch and gasped. Something wasn't right with Wren. She acted like I was about to hit her for putting her dish in the sink. "You don't have to run back to your room. I thought maybe we could go to the mall today. Kind of like a girls' day."

She gave me a small smile and shook her head. "Um, I kind of have a headache right now. Knock on my door when you're ready to go, and I'll see if I'm feeling any better." Wren dashed from the kitchen, almost bumping into Pipe who quickly stepped out of her way before she barreled into him.

"Was it something I said?" Karmen asked.

Cora shook her head and grabbed her empty plate. "No, it's not you. Hell, it doesn't have anything to do with us. Well, maybe Pipe and Maniac, but that's just because they're guys."

Maniac leaned against the counter by the fridge and crossed his arms over his chest. "What the hell does that mean?" he asked.

Pipe cleared his throat. "Unfortunately, I think it means the guys in Wren's past haven't treated her right."

"That fucking true?" Maniac demanded.

Cora dropped her plate in the sink and wiped her hands on her pants. "I don't know everything, but yeah, Wren hasn't had the best relationships. This last asshole really fucked with her."

Maniac pushed off the counter. "I'm not gonna fucking hurt her, dammit. She doesn't need to act like that around me."

"Calm down, brother," Pipe called. "We all know you haven't done anything to Wren."

"I'm gonna go get dressed and talk to her. Hopefully, she decides to go to the mall with us. She hasn't been out of the clubhouse since she got here, and I'm kind of worried about her." Cora followed Wren, and we were all speechless.

"Um, well, that majorly blows," Karmen sniffled. She wiped her nose with the back of her hand and pushed her half-empty plate away.

Nickel walked in and skidded to a halt. "Who the hell died?" he asked.

"We have to fix Wren," Karmen sobbed.

"What the hell did I miss?" he asked Pipe.

Pipe cleared his throat. "Not really sure, but from what I'm gathering, Wren's ex was a bigger dick than we thought."

Maniac pushed off the counter and paced back and forth. "I gotta go for a ride," he mumbled. "Can you guys keep an eye on Wren until I get back?"

"I really doubt she's going to leave her room, so I think you're good," Karmen replied.

"I was talking to Pipe and Nickel."

"Oh," Karmen gulped. "I suppose they are more likely to defend her than I am."

"You're good, brother," Pipe replied. "You can take off for the day if you want."

Maniac nodded. "I'll let you know what I'm up to. Right now, I need to just clear my head for a bit. Everything I thought I knew just got blew out of the water."

"What the hell was that?" Karmen asked after Maniac left the kitchen.

"I think that was us witnessing first-hand that Maniac might have a thing for Wren." Pipe wrapped his arm around my shoulders and pulled me close. "You okay?"

I looked up at him and nodded. "Yeah, I'm good. Worried about Wren, but I really doubt she'll talk to me seeing as I met her yesterday."

"Cora's got her, sugar, and I have a feeling Maniac just got a lot more involved than I bet he thought he would have." He pressed a kiss to the side of my head, and I went back to cracking eggs.

"How much fucking hot sauce did you put on that?"

I turned around to see Nickel waving his hand in front of his mouth and grabbing Karmen's cup of coffee.

"Well, from the pink tinge that the eggs have on them, I would say a shit ton," Alice smirked.

"Are you insane, woman?" Nickel finished Karmen's coffee and reached for Alice's.

Alice snatched it off the table and glared at Nickel. "Try it, and I break your hand."

Nickel pulled his hand back. "I see you have a nice sunny disposition in the morning just like Karmen."

As Karmen pulled the plate back in front of her she snatched the fork from Nickel. "Just for that, you don't get any more eggs."

"Promise?" Nickel laughed. "Pretty sure you're gonna be burping up fire after you finish that plate."

"But it's such a delicious burn," Karmen muttered.

Pipe pulled his lighter out of his pocket, and I glared at him. "You don't need that."

He shook his head and lit the end. "You'll have to keep my mouth occupied, sugar, if you don't want me to smoke anymore."

I rolled my eyes. "I'm buying you the patch today."

He shook his head and then turned it to exhale. At least the man had enough decency to turn his head. It would have been better if he didn't smoke at all, but I had to pick my battles at the moment.

"You buy me the patch, and you'll be wasting your money, sugar."

"You make me roll my eyes entirely too much," I mumbled. I finished cracking the eggs and grabbed another pound of bacon from the fridge.

"That's your sassy side coming out. I like it."

"You would," Nickel piped in. "When Karmen gets mouthy, it makes me think of all the other things she could be doing with her mouth instead of talking back."

Karmen pointed her fork at Nickel. "Keep it up, and I'll show you what else I can do with my fork."

Pipe busted out laughing, and Nickel held up his hands. "Point made, baby girl."

"You're looking a little green over there, Alice," Pipe chuckled.

Alice groaned and laid her head down on the table. "I can't decide if I need to throw up or eat."

"Ah, the aftereffects of a night with the Fallen Lords," Pipe chuckled.

"I remember when Pipe and Wrecker got me drunk," Karmen reminded. "That's when I became Captain."

"I remember you letting me shiver your timbers that night." Nickel wiggled his eyebrows.

Karmen elbowed him in the stomach and pushed her plate away again. "Pretty sure all of that hot sauce was a mistake." She rubbed her belly and laid her head on the counter like Alice.

"No one shivered my timbers last night," Alice grumbled.

"What in the hell is going on in here?" Wrecker asked. He walked into the kitchen and skidded to a halt just like Nickel had.

Pipe pointed at Karmen. "Too much hot sauce eggs." Then shifted to Nickel. "Ate the hot sauce eggs without knowing that they were hot sauce eggs," then finally landed on Alice. "Partied with the Fallen Lords last night."

Wrecker nodded like that all made sense to him. "Sounds like a typical morning when you ladies are around." Wrecker grabbed a cup down from the cabinet and filled it up. "Where are Maniac and Wren?"

"Um, Wren is in her room with Cora," I mumbled.

"Maniac is gone for the day," I added.

"What the fuck do you mean he's gone for the day?" Wrecker demanded. "That asshole's job is to watch Wren." Wrecker pulled out a chair neck to Nickel and sat down. Alice groaned when he bumped the table, but she didn't raise her head.

"Cora told us some information about Wren today that none of us knew. Kind of threw Maniac off a bit," Nickel explained.

"You wanna tell me exactly what that information was?"

I started laying the bacon into the pan and waited to hear who was going to explain about Wren.

Pipe cleared his throat. "Don't know a lot of the details, but Nikki touched her, and she froze. Like deer in the headlights, spooked."

"Oh Jesus," Wrecker grumbled. "Please don't say it."

"Don't know for sure what is going on with her, but Cora said she was pretty messed up from her relationship with the fucker from the Hell Captains."

Wrecker slammed his hand down on the table. "Not only do I have huge fucking shit brewing all around us, now we gotta deal with this. I'd like one fucking day where we don't get shit on more and more." Wrecker stormed out of the kitchen, and the only noise was the sizzling of the bacon in the pan.

Alice raised her head, and Karmen leaned into Nickel.

Pipe's eyes fell on me, and I tried to plaster on a smile.

Pipe put his arm around my shoulders and pulled me close. "It'll all be okay, sugar."

"I hope you're right," I mumbled.

Wrecker was right, and I only knew about two things that were happening with the Fallen Lords right now. I could only imagine what else was going on.

*

Chapter 31

Pipe

"I need you back here."

I rested my hands on the table and looked at my brothers that were gathered around the table. "I know. I need a couple of weeks to get Nikki on board. I can't leave her in Kales Corners by herself."

"I'm not asking you to leave your woman there. I'm telling you to pack your shit up, your woman included, and be fucking present. Playtime is over." Wrecker leaned forward. "Brinks is finding out info about The Ultra and Oakley. I need you here to take the reins while I travel to where Oakley lives and get our decoy in place."

"When are you leaving?" I asked.

"A week from Thursday."

That gave me nine days to talk to Nikki and convince her we needed to move back to Weston. "I'll be back Wednesday." Make that eight days.

Wrecker nodded his head, satisfied. "Now onto Wren and the Hell Captains."

"I say we just blow their fucking clubhouse up and be done with the fucking assholes," Maniac growled.

"You would suggest blowing them up," Nickel laughed. "Maybe you could throw a couple of fireworks in there to pretty it up."

"Totally doable," Maniac bragged.

After Maniac had taken off all day, he was back to the clubhouse right when Nickel and I had returned with the girls from the mall. Also known as Hell on Earth. Cora and Wren had stayed back with Brinks and Slayer keeping an eye on them while Nikki, Karmen, and Alice dragged Nickel and me into every damn store.

Maniac had seemed different after his ride. There was an edge to him that he never had before. Wren being abused by her ex was weighing heavily on him.

"Not happening," Wrecker vetoed. "As much as I would like to see the maggots disappear, obliterating a whole club seems a bit drastic."

Maniac shrugged. "Then what exactly do you have in mind?"

"We just get rid of the ones causing us problems." Wrecker looked at Brinks. "Add finding out which one Wren was dating to your list of shit to look up."

Brinks shook his head. "Not like I was doing anything else."

"You got a problem?" Wrecker thundered.

Brinks held up his hands. "Nah, it's just that don't you think you could task someone else to dig up shit on them? The Ultra is taking up all of my time."

Wrecker growled. "Pardon me for overloading you. Find out who the boyfriend was."

It never was a good idea to question Wrecker. He normally gave one chance to listen, and if you didn't hear him, he would *make* you listen.

Wrecker slammed the gavel on the table and stormed out of church.

"Am I the only noticing Wrecker is a bit on edge lately?" Boink asked. "Storming out of the room seems to be his M.O. lately."

"Why don't you point that out to him, Boink? I'm sure that will help the situation." Nickel flicked him upside the head and turned to me. "You really think you'll be back in Weston that soon?"

I shrugged and stood up. "I don't have much of a choice. The club needs me, and the only thing that is keeping me in Kales Corners is Nikki, and she's going to have to understand."

"You really are new at this couple shit, aren't you?" Nickel shook his head. "Telling Nikki she *has* to move is not an option."

"Well, Nickel, I have eight fucking days. Explain to me how I'm going to get her to move with actually *telling* her we're moving?"

He sat back and crossed his arms over his head. "Gotta make her think it was her idea, brother. That's the only way you are going to make this happen smoothly."

Yeah, that sounded as easy as getting an elephant in a tutu.

Fucking impossible.

"Just let me worry about it. I'll be back Wednesday. Try not to make Wrecker's head explode before then." All the guys grumbled, but they knew not to bitch and moan. I made my way out of church and out to my truck.

Nikki and Alice were saying goodbye to Cora and Karmen, and then we were headed back to Kales Corners.

I heard the roar of a bike and knew that Wrecker had taken off, frustrated over all the shit going on. I couldn't blame the guy for disappearing for a bit.

At least Slayer and Brinks had returned this morning and reported that they had a chat with Richard and were convinced that he wasn't going to be a problem anymore.

Nikki was upset that I had been right that he was the one watching her, but she was glad that he was going to stop and he hadn't been hurt.

At least that was what I had told her.

Two broken fingers wasn't really hurting him anyway. The way I looked at it, the guy got off easy.

"Time to hit the road," I called as I stepped outside.

"Call me when you get home," Karmen told Nikki. 'And don't forget to think about what we talked about."

Nikki ducked her head and mumbled something I couldn't make out. What in the hell were these two up to again?

"Alice, make sure you drink a shit ton of water when you get home. I'm pretty sure you're gonna have a two-day hangover which we all know is worse the second day."

Alice gave her a two-finger salute and crawled into the truck. I didn't know who she partied with last night, but she definitely tied one on.

Karmen pointed her finger at me. "Take care of my best friend."

Jesus, this chick was crazy. "I plan on it, Captain."

Karmen flipped me off and stepped back next to Cora. Apparently, Wren still wasn't up to coming out of her room.

Maniac was going to have his hands full with that one.

"You guys got all your shit?" I asked as I backed up.

Alice groaned in the back and raised her thumb.

"I think I got everything. We'll be back soon anyway, right?"

I looked over at Nikki and smiled. "Yeah, we will be, sugar."

Maybe convincing Nikki to move back to Weston wasn't going to be as hard as I thought.

*

Chapter 32

Nikki

"I'm just gonna check on my side of the duplex to make sure Brinks and Slayer didn't destroy it."

I groaned and slid out of the truck. "While you do that, I'm gonna hop in the shower."

"Just wait for me, sugar."

I wrapped my arms around his neck and pressed a kiss to his lips. "How about you check on the duplex, and I'll get all soapy in the shower so you can help rinse me off," I purred. I was more than excited to be home and have Pipe all to myself.

"Now that sounds like a damn good idea," he growled.

"I tend to have them every now and then."

I pulled him to the front door and stepped to the side so he could unlock the door. "You better be naked and ready by the time I get in there."

My fingers trailed along his chest, and I pressed a quick kiss to his lips. "I'll be more than ready."

Pipe pushed off the side of the house and jogged over to the other side of the duplex. "I want you wet, sugar," he called.

Mission accomplished.

I closed the door and pulled my shirt over my head. The sooner I got undressed, the sooner I would be in the shower waiting for Pipe.

My shoes were toed off at the door, my shirt on top of them, and my pants hit the floor halfway to the bathroom.

After I turned on the water, I reached behind me to unhook my bra and heard footsteps in the living room. "No fair," I called. "You were way quicker than I thought you would have been." My fingers fumbled with the clasp, and I took a step toward the door. "You think you can get this for me? You've got me too excited."

I felt Pipe move behind me and his fingers were on my back. "I'm glad to see that you're ready for me, Nikki." The blood rushed from my face, and thick fingers wrapped around my neck. "Time to really make you mine now."

I gagged against the hold on my neck, and stars flashed in front of me. "Please," I gasped.

"The time for begging is over. You never should have sent those white trash bikers after me, Nikki. Things never end well when I'm threatened."

He squeezed my neck harder and pulled me against his body. "Everything you let that biker do to you, I'm going to do now. I figured as soon as I agreed that I would leave you alone that he would disappear." He leaned down and pressed his lips against my ear. "I was right," he whispered.

"Richard, please." My fingers clawed at his hand around my neck, but he didn't let me go.

"Keep struggling, I like it." His other hand circled around my waist, and he laid his hand on my mound. He pressed against me and ground his hard dick against me.

"Please, please, don't do this."

Richard tsked. "I like when they struggle, but I hate when they talk," he mumbled. "But I forgot my bag, so we're going to have to decide what to do. The struggle is nice, but I can't stand the talking," he mumbled out loud.

His hand left my body, and he reached for something behind him. "Nighty, night, Nikki. This won't hurt a bit."

I opened my mouth to scream when his body moved from mine, but everything went dark, and I didn't feel anything anymore.

*

Chapter 33

Pipe

I would never understand how Brinks and Slayer managed to make that place an even bigger hell hole.

Four empty pizza boxes were stacked on the kitchen counter, at least fifteen beer cans were littered around the living room, and the mysterious brown stain on the living room carpet seemed to have grown. A lot.

Thoughts of Nikki naked and wet in the shower outweighed taking the time to clean up. The mess would still be here after I thoroughly fucked Nikki. Twice.

I grabbed a clean shirt and a pair of boxers from my dresser and headed over to Nikki's side of the duplex. I pulled my door shut behind me, locked it, and noticed Nikki's door was wide open.

"What the fuck," I mumbled. I sidestepped to her door and listened. All I could hear was the sound of the shower, but something wasn't right. I looked around, wishing that I hadn't left my gun next door, and remembered I had a piece of pipe in the back of my truck.

I gripped the pipe in my hand, thankful that I hadn't cleaned out the back of my truck, and slinked back over to the front door.

Nikki's clothes were littered on the floor, her usual trail she made to the bathroom.

"Fucking heavy, bitch."

My blood ran cold, and I clenched my fists. He had Nikki. That fucking cocksucker.

I plastered myself against the hallway wall and sidestepped down it. I peeked around the corner and saw the bathroom was empty, but the bathroom mat was scrunched up against the side of the tub, and there was a bloody handprint on the counter.

I closed my eyes and took a deep breath. She was okay. She had to be okay. I tightened my grip on the pipe and moved toward the bedroom. I heard Richard before I saw him. He was grunting and groaning all while I assumed he was trying to get Nikki on the bed.

"Never should have hit her over the head," he grumbled. "Or I should have at least waited until she was on the bed."

The guy was a fucking whack job. I made it to the doorway, looked into the bedroom, and saw Nikki's body lying limply half on the bed.

I was gonna kill the fucker.

My gaze ran over him, making sure he didn't have a weapon or anything on him that he could use against me.

He grabbed her leg and yanked her onto the bed, and a groan came from her mouth.

I breathed a sigh of relief and closed my eyes for a second. Thank God she was alive.

"Quiet, bitch," he grunted. "Don't make me hit you again. As soon as I get you on this bed, I'm going to give you exactly what you need."

"No," Nikki groaned. "Please."

I soundlessly crept into the room, and my eyes connected with Nikki's. I put a finger to my lips and shook my head so she wouldn't alert Richard that I was in the room.

She groaned and closed her eyes, knowing that all of this was going to be over soon.

"Hey cocksucker," I boomed.

Richard spun around, surprise on his face. "What the hell are you doing here?" he demanded like I was the one in the wrong.

Mother fucker was gonna pay. "I got the same question for you."

"You don't fucking deserve her," he spit out.

"I know I fucking don't, but I'm a selfish bastard, and I'm going to work for her 'til I fucking die."

Richard opened his mouth, but I wasn't going to listen to him anymore.

I reared back, lifting the pipe over my head, and swung, connecting with the nutjob's head. Nikki screamed, and I heard the crushing of his skull as I swung with all my might. His body lifted off the floor with the force of the blow, and then he landed on the floor like a ragdoll.

"Oh, my God," Nikki screamed.

I dropped the pipe at my feet and gathered Nikki in my arms. "Where are you hurt?" I demanded. I ran my hands over her body, but I couldn't find any blood from the handprint in the bathroom. "Where are you bleeding?"

Nikki groaned and laid her head on my shoulder. "I don't think I'm bleeding. He hit me over the head pretty hard, but I don't think he broke the skin."

I cradled her head in my hands and looked down at her. "There was blood in the bathroom, sugar. Where did it come from?"

She shook her head and closed her eyes. "It's not mine," she mumbled.

"Stay awake for me, Nikki. You can't go to sleep right now." My fingers gently probed her head and felt a huge goose egg on the side of it. "What did he hit you with, sugar?"

She opened her eyes, and a loopy smile spread across her lips. "I don't want to tell you because then you'll say that you were right."

Even banged up and concussed, Nikki still had sass to throw around. "I'm not gonna brag. Just tell me what he hit you with."

"My damn blow dryer you always complain about me never putting away."

I closed my eyes and sighed. She was right, I was totally going to give her hell over that, but not until I knew that she was okay. I pulled my phone out of my pocket and quickly called nine-one-one.

The dispatcher told me a car and ambulance were on the way and should be here shortly. I tossed the phone on the bed and looked down at Richard.

"Did you kill him?" Nikki asked meekly. She looked at his limp body and grimaced.

"No, he's still breathing." His chest shifted up and down, but he wasn't moving. When he did finally wake up, he was going to have one hell of a headache.

"Where did you get a pipe from?"

"It was in the back of my truck."

She laid her head on my shoulder and sighed. "I think I know how you got the name Pipe now." She was right about that.

Her eyes closed, and I cradled her cheek. "Open your eyes for me, sugar." She opened one eye and looked up at me.

"I'm naked, aren't I?" she whispered.

"Yeah, but you're okay." I didn't want to ask the question, but I needed to know. "He didn't touch you or anything, did he?"

She gently shook her head and grimaced. "No. At least not in a way to get his rocks off. He hit me over the head, but he didn't have enough time to do anything before you came in."

I breathed a sigh of relief. "Are you okay to put a shirt on?" As much as I knew I shouldn't move her in case there was something more wrong with her, I wasn't fond of the idea of anyone seeing her topless. Her panties were still on, but she must have taken her bra off before Richard hit her.

"I'm fine. My head just hurts a bit." I laid her back onto the bed, sliding a pillow under her head, and grabbed a shirt out of her dresser. "Can you sit up for two seconds?"

She closed her eyes and nodded. "Yeah."

I hated seeing her like this. My strong, beautiful, passionate Nikki was beaten and hurt, and there was nothing I could do to help her.

She swung her legs over the bed, and I squatted in front of her. "Easy, sugar." She put her hands on my shoulders and smiled. "Thank you for saving me," she whispered.

"I fucking love you, Nikki," I croaked. I couldn't go another second without her knowing. "I'm pretty sure I fell in love with you the first time you smiled at me, but I was too stupid to realize it."

"You were pretty stupid," she laughed.

"Even with a concussion, you still give me shit."

"It's all part of my charm." She gave me a wonky wink and tilted her head to the side. "My head really hurts, but I have to tell you I love you too before I pass out. I'm not stupid and knew I loved you after you took off my underwear." She closed her eyes and giggled. "That sounded way more romantic in my head."

"It sounded pretty good to me, sugar." She loved me. Holy shit, she loved me.

Sirens sounded in the distance, snapping me out of my stupor. "Let's get this shirt on you so you can go for a ride in the ambulance."

Her eyes snapped open, and a goofy grin spread across her lips. "That sounds like fun. Do you think they'll let you lay down with me in the abulancey?"

I chuckled and slipped the shirt over her head. "Feeling a little woozy?"

She nodded her head and grimaced. "Just a bit."

I put her arms into the holes and pulled the shirt over her body. "I should be able to ride with you in the ambulance, but I don't think I'll be able to lay down with you."

She leaned forward and rested her head on my shoulder. "Major bummer," she mumbled.

A loud knock sounded on the door, and I hollered that we were in the bedroom.

The EMT's worked on Nikki first. They loaded her onto the stretcher, and asked her fifty questions, and then rolled her out of the room. The police had called for a second ambulance when they saw that Richard was injured too, and they showed up as Nikki was being wheeled out.

They were working on Richard when the cop pulled me out of the room and asked for a quick rundown of what had occurred. It was obvious to see what had happened, but I understood they needed to get facts straight.

I managed to jump in the back of the ambulance before they closed the doors. "Pipe," Nikki gasped. "I was afraid you were going to have to stay."

I probably should have, but I didn't want to leave Nikki. "I'll never leave you, sugar."

Nikki babbled the whole way on the short ride to the hospital even though her eyes were closed the whole time. She insisted she wasn't tired, but the light hurt her eyes. The EMT said that was common with concussions and reassured me that it was a good sign that she was coherent and talking.

By the time we were in a room, and a doctor had looked her over, Nikki was fading fast.

"Are you sure I can sleep? I always thought you're not supposed to sleep when you have a concussion," she mumbled.

I pulled a chair up to her bed and threaded my fingers through hers. "That's why they got you hooked up like a car battery right now. They're monitoring everything, so if you do fall asleep, they can still check on you."

She closed her eyes and smiled. "Did you really say you loved me before, or did I imagine that?"

I sat back and squeezed her hand. "I said it then, and I'll say it again. I love you, sugar."

She sighed and opened her eyes. "Would you still love me if I said I never want to step foot in that duplex again?"

I laughed and stroked the back of her hand with my thumb. "I'm pretty sure that's reasonable."

"Can we move back to Weston? I love Kales Corners, Alice, and Bos, but I miss Weston."

"Sugar, maybe you should try to get some sleep, and we can talk about this in the morning."

She shook her head and tried to sit up. I put a hand on her arm, and leaned forward, holding her down.

"Nikki, calm down."

"I am calm. I just need to know that we're moving back to Weston. That's what Karmen was talking about when she said I needed to just talk to you. I wanted to move back before this whole mess. I saw how you were in Weston, and how much the club means to you. I didn't want to be the reason why you weren't there."

I reached up and brushed her hair from her eyes. "I want the club, but I want you too."

"And you can have both in Weston. I like my job at the diner, but I loved my job at the nursing home. I miss home."

"I should probably tell you that Wrecker told me I had to be back in Weston in eight days, and I was racking my brain trying to figure out how to get you back there with me."

She smiled and laid back down. "Dodged a bullet with that one, didn't you?"

I sat back and smirked. "You have no idea, sugar. Nickel told me I had to make you think it was your idea to move."

Her eyes bugged out. "Karmen told me the same thing when we were dancing around each other. Told me I had to call the shots but make you think that you were."

"And you think you did that?"

She closed her eyes. "You did fall in love with me the first time I smiled at you, so you tell me?" She sighed deeply and nestled into her pillow. "I'm gonna sleep now. Promise you won't leave?"

I squeezed her hand and shifted my chair closer to her bed. "I'll never leave you, Nikki."

*

Chapter 34

Nikki

Seven Days Later

"Holy crap. This place is huge."

I set the box of dishes on the counter and looked at Alice who was carrying a pile of blankets in her arms. "You couldn't carry anything heavier?" I laughed.

She tossed them on the couch that was in the middle of the living room and shook her head. "Someone had to take them. No reason why that someone shouldn't have been me."

Karmen walked through the front door with a pillow under one arm and a bottle of water in the other. "Nickel has banished me from carrying anything. He said I'm just supposed to direct." She plopped down on the sofa and kicked her feet up. "I still can't believe your luck with getting this house. It's a mile from the clubhouse, and the rent is dirt cheap."

Alice sat down and put her arm around Karmen's shoulders. "And there's an extra bedroom for the weekends I decide I want to party with the Fallen Lords."

"I see you've forgotten last time when you were a walking zombie the day after."

Alice scoffed. "It really wasn't that bad. Besides, I don't know when my next weekend off is going to be since a waitress quit on us with no notice."

I rolled my eyes and started unpacking dishes. "I told Bos that I would stay on until he found someone else, but he insisted that you guys would be fine."

"He feels guilty about Richard."

"What? Why on Earth would he feel guilty about that?"

"Because he said he would have done something about him years ago, but everyone just swept it under the rug."

"The whack job is the only one responsible for his actions," Karmen pointed out. "Thankfully, Pipe was there, otherwise, who knows what would have happened. I'm three months pregnant and so not up to looking for a new best friend."

I grabbed a stack of plates and put them in the cabinet. "I'm so glad you're worried about my well-being, Karmen. I'm sure it would have been a chore to find a new best friend."

"You have no idea," she sighed.

"Are Cora and Wren coming over?" Alice asked.

"Cora texted that she was on the way over, but not Wren. Something about she knocked, but Wren didn't answer," Karmen answered.

"I hope everything is okay with Wren. I really liked hanging out with her," I mused.

"She had to be fine. I told Cora that Wren is officially part of the Girl Gang so she can't keep skipping out on meetings anymore."

"Wait," I turned around and looked at Karmen. "What meetings?"

"The one we're having right now."

Alice looked at me and tilted her head. "Does that make me a Girl Gang Nomad because I live an hour away."

Karmen squealed. "Oh, my God, it totally does! You're the first Girl Gang Nomad!"

"What the hell is all the screaming about in here?" Pipe asked. He was carrying three boxes in his arms, and Nickel was behind him carrying the same.

"Just Girl Gang stuff."

Nickel rolled his eyes and set the boxes next to the couch. "You're a nut, woman. You think since I'm part of an MC you need to have your own group too?" he chuckled.

Karmen shrugged. "Hey, I can have a little fun too."

"Is that what they're calling crazy these days, fun?" Pipe asked. Karmen threw a pillow at him, and he caught it mid-air. "Nice try, darlin'."

She flipped him off and crossed her arms over her chest. "Be thankful I'm pregnant, or I'd totally take you down right now, dick."

Alice and Karmen high-fived and tossed another pillow at Pipe. This one hit him squarely in the back, because he was headed straight for me and didn't stop 'til he wrapped me in his arms. "Your girls are crazy, sugar."

"Yeah, they are," I agreed. I wrapped my arms around his waist and looked around our house. "I still can't believe we got this place."

"Perfect timing, sugar."

I leaned back and looked up at him. "I guess you're right. When we first met, we didn't have the timing thing right, but now we got it just right."

He pressed a kiss to my lips and smiled. "All it took was for me to pull my head out of my ass and realize what was right in front of me. I love you, Nikki."

"I love you too, Pipe, because you are the only person I know who can make me swoon by talking about pulling their head out of their ass."

"What can I say, you bring it out of me, sugar."

I leaned my head against his shoulder and sighed.

It may have taken moving to a new town and running from the man I loved, but it all worked out in the end.

Pipe loved me, and that was all I could ask for.

*

Chapter 35

Maniac

I pounded on the door again, but she didn't answer. Normally by the third time I knocked, she threw open the door and asked me what the hell I wanted.

Something wasn't right.

"Wren, open the goddamn door," I hollered.

Brinks peeked his head out of his room and smirked. "Trouble in paradise?" he asked.

"Something isn't right, man." I tried turning the doorknob, but she had it locked.

"You break down that door, you know Wrecker is going to string you up by your nuts," Brinks reminded me.

I pounded on the door. I waited ten seconds and looked at Brinks. Fuck it.

Wrecker could make me pay for the damn door, I didn't give a fuck.

I stepped back and powered into the door. My shoulder made contact and busted through. "Wren," I called when I didn't see her on the bed.

The water in the tub was running, and I was going to look like a complete ass if she was just taking a bath and didn't hear me.

"Wren," I called again.

She should have heard me though. Hell, everyone in the clubhouse probably heard me.

I cautiously moved to the open bathroom door and called her name again.

I made it to the door and went numb. Everything went silent as I watched Wren float in the water.

Water tinted pink from the blood seeping from her wrists.

The End

Coming Soon:

Black Belt Knockout, book 4 in the Powerhouse M.A. series.

January 2018

Maniac, book 3 in the Fallen Lords MC series.

March 2018

About the Author

Winter Travers is a devoted wife, mother, and aunt turned author who was born and raised in Wisconsin. After a brief stint in South Carolina following her heart to chase the man who is now her hubby, they retreated back up North to the changing seasons, and to the place they now call home.

Winter spends her days writing happily ever after's, and her nights zipping around on her forklift at work. She also has an addiction to anything MC related, her dog Thunder, and Mexican food! (Tamales!)

Winter loves to stay connected with her readers. Don't hesitate to reach out and contact her.

www.facebook.com/wintertravers

Twitter: @WinterTravers

Instagram: @WinterTravers

http://500145315.wix.com/wintertravers

LOVING LO

DEVIL'S KNIGHTS SERIES

BOOK 1

WINTER TRAVERS

Chapter 1

Meg

How did just stopping quickly to get dog food and shampoo turn into an overflowing basket and a surplus pack of paper towels?

"Put the paper towels down and back away slowly," I mumbled to myself as I walked past a display of air fresheners and wondered if I needed any.

"Oh dear. Oh, my. I… Ah… Oh, my."

I tore my thoughts away from air fresheners and looked down the aisle to an elderly woman who was leaning against the shelf, fanning herself. "Are you ok, ma'am?"

"Oh dear. I just… I just got a little… dizzy." I looked at the woman and saw her hands shaking as she brushed her white hair out of her face. The woman had on denim capris and a white button down short sleeve shirt and surprisingly three-inch wedge heels.

"Ok, well, why don't we try to find you a place to sit down until you get your bearings?" I shifted the basket and paper towels under one arm to help

227

her to the bench that I had seen by the shoe rack two aisles over. "Are you here with anyone?" I asked, as I guided her down the aisle.

"Oh no. I'm here by myself. I just needed a few things."

"I only needed two things, and now my basket is overflowing, and I still haven't gotten the things I came in for."

The woman plopped down on the bench chuckling, shaking her head. "Tell me about it. Happens to me every time too."

"Is there something I can do for you? Has this happened to you before?" She was looking rather pale.

"Unfortunately, yes. I ran out of the house today without eating breakfast. I'm diabetic. I should know by now that I can't do that." My mom was also diabetic, so I knew exactly what the woman was talking about. Luckily, I also knew what to do to help.

"Just sit right here, and I'll be right back. Is there someone you want to call to give you a ride home? Driving right now probably isn't the best idea." I set the basket and towels on the floor, keeping my wallet in my hand.

"I suppose I should call my son. He should be able to give me a ride," the woman said as she dug her phone out of her purse.

I left the woman to her phone call and headed to the candy aisle that I had been trying to ignore. I grabbed a bag of licorice, chips, and a diet soda and went to the checkout. The dollar store didn't offer a healthy selection, but this would do in a pinch. The woman just needed to get her blood sugars back up.

I grabbed my things after paying and headed back to the bench. I ripped open the bag and handed it to the woman. "Oh dear, you didn't have to buy that. I could have given you money."

"Don't worry about it. I hope if this happened to my mom there would be someone to help her if I wasn't around."

"Well, that's awfully sweet of you. My names Ethel Birch by the way."

"It's nice to meet you, Ethel. I'm Meg Grain. I also got you some chips and soda." I popped opened the soda and handed it to Ethel.

"Oh, thank you, honey. My son is on the way here, should be only five minutes. You can get going if you want to, you don't need to sit with an old woman," Ethel said as she ate a piece of candy and took a slug of soda.

"No problem. The only plans I had today was to take a nap before work tonight. Delaying my plans by ten minutes won't be a problem."

"Well, in that case, you can help me eat this licorice. It's my favorite, but I shouldn't eat this all by myself. Where do you work at?" Ethel asked as she offered the bag to me.

"The factory right outside of town. I work in the warehouse, second shift." I grabbed a piece and sat down on the floor. If I was going to wait for Ethel's son to show up, might as well be comfortable while I waited for him.

"Really? Never would have thought that. Figured you would have said a nurse or something like that. Seems like you would have to be tough to work in a warehouse, sounds like a man's job."

I laughed. "Honestly, Ethel that is not the first time I have heard that, and it probably won't be the last. You need a certain attitude to deal with those truckers walking through the door. I have an awesome co-worker, so he helps out when truckers have a problem with a woman loading their truck."

"Sounds like you give them hell. My Tim was a trucker before he passed. I know exactly what you are talking about." Ethel took another drink of her soda and set it on the bench next to her.

"Feeling better?"

"Surprisingly, yes. It's a wonder what a little candy can do. How much do I owe you?" Ethel asked as she reached for her purse by her feet.

"Don't worry about it. I'm just glad that I was here to help."

"Mom! Where are you?" Someone yelled from the front of the store.

"Oh good, Lo's here. You'll have to meet him." Ethel cupped her hands around her mouth and yelled to him she was in the back.

I started getting up off the floor and remembered I wasn't exactly as flexible as I use to be while struggling to get up.

"Ma, you ok?" I was halfway to standing with my butt in the air when his voice made me pause.

It sounded like the man was gurgling broken glass when he spoke. Raspy and *so* sexy. Those three words he spoke sent shocks to my core. Lord knows the last time I felt anything in my core.

"Yes, I'm fine. I forgot to eat breakfast this morning and started to get dizzy when Meg here was nice enough to help me out until you could get here." Ethel turned to me. "Lo, this is Meg, Meg this is Lo."

Oh, lord.

I couldn't talk. The man standing in front of me was... oh, lord. I couldn't even think of a word to describe him.

I looked him up and down, and I'm sure my mouth was hanging wide open. I took in his scuffed up motorcycle boots and faded, stained ripped jeans that hugged his thighs and made me want to ask the man to spin so I could see what those jeans were doing for his ass. I moved my eyes up to his t-shirt that was tight around his shoulders and chest and showed he worked out.

I couldn't remember the last time I worked out. Did walking to the mailbox count as exercise? Of course, I only remembered to get the mail about twice a week, so that probably didn't count.

His arms were covered in tattoos. I could see them peeking out from the collar of his shirt and could only imagine what he looked like with his shirt off. Tattoos were my ultimate addiction on a man. Even one tattoo added at least 10 points to a man's hotness. This guy was off the fucking charts.

My eyes locked with his after my fantastic voyage up his body, and I stopped breathing.

"Hey, Meg. See something you like, darlin'?" Lo rumbled at me with a smirk on his face.

Busted. I sucked air back into my lungs and tried to remember how to breathe.

Lo's eyes were the color of fresh cut grass, bright green. His hair was jet black and cut close to his head with a pair of kick ass aviators sitting on top of his head. He was golden tan and gorgeous. The man was sex on a stick. Plain and simple.

"Uh, hey," I choked out.

Lo's lips curved up into a grin, and I looked down to see if my panties fell off. The man had a panty-dropping smile, and he wasn't even smiling that big. I would have to take cover or risk fainting if he smiled any bigger.

"Thanks for looking after my ma for me. I'm glad I was in town today and not out on a run," Lo said.

Ok. Get it together Meg. You are a 36-year-old woman, and this man has rendered you speechless like a sixteen-year-old girl. I needed to say something.

"Say something," I blurted out. Good Lord did I just say that. Lo quirked his eyebrow, and his smirk returned.

"Ugh, I mean no problem. I didn't do that much. No problem." I looked at Ethel while Lo was smirking at me; Ethel had a full-blown smile on her face and was beaming at me.

"You were a life saver, Meg! I don't know what I would have done if you weren't here." Ethel looked at Lo and grinned even bigger. "You should have seen her, Lo. She knew just what to do to help me. I could have sworn she was a nurse the way she took charge. She's not, though, just has a good head on her shoulders and decided to help this old lady out."

"That's good, Ma. You got all your shit you need so we can get going? I got some stuff going on at the garage that I dropped to get over here fast."

I took that as my cue to leave and ripped my eyes off Lo and bent over to get my basket and paper towels.

"Yes son, that's my stuff right here. I just want to get Meg's number before she leaves."

"Why do you need my number?" I asked, as I juggled my basket and towels.

Ethel grabbed her purse off the ground and started digging through it again. "Well, you won't let me pay you back for the snacks you got for me so I figured I could pay you back by inviting you over for dinner sometime. So, what's your number, sweetheart?"

"I don't eat dinner," I blurted out. I was going to have to have a talk with my brain and mouth when I got home. They needed to get their shit together and start working in unison so I wouldn't sound like such an idiot.

"You don't eat dinner? Please don't tell me you're on a diet." Lo said as he looked me up and down.

"No," I said. Lord knew I should be.

Lo and Ethel just stared at me.

"So, no, you don't eat dinner?" Lo asked again.

"Yes. I mean no, I'm not on a diet. Yes, I eat dinner. I just work at night, so I meant that I wouldn't be able to come to dinner." I looked at Lo and blushed about ten shades of red. "Why is this so hard?"

"What's hard, sweetheart? Can't remember your phone number? I can barely remember mine too. Don't worry about not being able to make it to dinner; I can have you over for lunch. You eat lunch right?" Ethel asked with a smirk on her face. Lo had a full-blown smile on his face, even his eyes were smiling at me. That smile ought to be illegal.

I could see where Lo got his looks from. With Lo and Ethel standing next to each other, I could totally see the resemblance. Especially when they were both smirking.

I had to get out of here. I'm normally the one with the one-liners and making everyone laugh, now I couldn't even put two words together.

"Lunch would be good." I rattled off my number, and Ethel jotted it down.

"Ok, sweetheart, I'll let you get your nap. I'll give you a call later, and we can figure out a day we can get together." Ethel shoved the pen and paper back in her bag and leaned into me for a hug.

I awkwardly hugged her back and patted her on the shoulder. "Sounds good. Have a good day, Ethel. Uh, it was nice meeting you, Lo," I mumbled, as my gaze wandered over Lo again.

"You too Meg. See you around," Lo replied.

I gave them both a jaunty wave and booked it to the checkout. Thankfully there wasn't a line, and I quickly made my escape to my car. I threw my things in the trunk and hopped in. I grabbed my phone out of my pocket and plugged it into the radio and turned on my chill playlist, as the soothing sounds of Fleetwood Mac filled the car.

Music was the one thing in my life that had gotten me through so much shit. Good or bad, there was always a song that I could play, and it would make everything better. Right now, I just needed to unscramble my brain and get my bearings. Fleetwood Mac singing "Landslide" was helping.

I pulled out of the parking lot and headed home. All I needed was to forget about today. If Ethel called for lunch, I would say yes because she did remind me so much of mom, but I wasn't going to let Lo enter my thoughts anymore. A woman like me did not register on his radar, he was better just forgotten.

When I was halfway home, I realized I forgot dog food and shampoo.

Shit.

======

Lo

I helped mom finish her shopping and loaded all her crap into the truck. I looked around the parking lot for Meg, hoping she hadn't left yet so I could get another look at her. As soon as I saw her ass waving in the air as she struggled to stand up, I knew I had to be inside her.

It took all my willpower to not get a hard-on as her eyes ran over my body. Fucking chick was smoking' hot and didn't even know it.

"Thanks for coming to get me, Lo," Ma said as she interrupted my thoughts about Meg.

"No problem, Ma. I'll get one of the guys to bring your car to you later. Make sure it's locked." Ma dug her keys out of her huge ass purse and beeped the locks. We both got into the shop truck, and I started it up.

"Sure was nice of that Meg to help out. I don't know what I would have done without her."

"Yup, definitely nice of her." I shifted the truck into drive, keeping my foot on the brake, knowing exactly where mom was headed with this.

"You should ask her out." All I could do was shake my head and laugh.

"Straight to the point huh, Ma?"

"I'm old, I can say what I want. Meg is just the thing you need."

"I didn't know I needed anything." I pulled out of the parking lot and headed to Ma's house.

"You need someone in your life besides that club." My mom grabbed her phone out of her purse and started fiddling with it.

"We'll see, ma. Meg didn't seem too thrilled with me." She liked what she saw, but it was like she couldn't get away from me quick enough when she saw that Ma was going to be ok.

"Well, you are pretty intimidating, Lo. Thank goodness you didn't wear your cut."

My leather vest with my club rockers and patches was a part of me. "What the hell is wrong with my cut? If some bitch can't handle me in my cut, she sure as shit doesn't belong with me," I growled.

"Not what I meant Lo. That girl has been hurt, you can see it in her eyes. You'll have to be gentle with her."

My phone dinged. I dug it out of my pocket and saw my mom had texted me. "You texted me her number, ma?"

"Use it, Logan, fix her," she insisted.

I sighed and pulled into mom's driveway. "Maybe she doesn't want to be fixed, ma. Maybe she has a boyfriend."

"She doesn't. Call her, or I'll do it for you," she ordered.

I knew my mom's threat wasn't idle. She totally would call Meg and ask her out for me. Fuck. "I'll help you get your shit inside, ma."

"I'll make you lunch, and then you can call Meg," Ma said, as she jumped out of the truck and grabbed some bags.

I watched her walk into her house and looked at the message she had sent me. I saved Meg's number to my phone and grabbed the rest of Ma's shit and headed into the house.

Looked like I was calling Meg.

=======

Take a ride with the Jensen Boys.

Meet Violet and Luke in the first chapter of DownShift!

DOWNSHIFT

SKID ROW KINGS

BOOK 1

WINTER TRAVERS

Chapter 1

Violet

It was half past seven, and I should be on my way home already, but I wasn't.

I watched the lone girl who was sitting at the far table and sighed. She came in every day after school like clockwork, stayed till five forty-five then left. Except today, she didn't. The only way for me to get the heck out of here was to tell her the library was closing, but I didn't have the heart to.

She appeared to be well taken care of, nice clothes, good tennis shoes and well groomed. But she was never with anyone when she came in. Even when other kids would come in to work on homework or such, she stayed by herself at the far table.

I glanced at the watch on my wrist one last time and knew I had to go talk to her. All I wanted to do was go home, eat dinner, and take a nice long bath with my latest book boyfriend. Was that too much to ask?

After I skirted around the desk, I hesitantly made my way over to her, not wanting to tell someone they had to leave. I wasn't one for confrontation. "Um, excuse me."

The girl looked up at me and smiled. She couldn't have been more than thirteen, fourteen tops. Shiny braces encased her teeth, and black-rimmed glasses sat perched on her nose. "Yes?"

"The library closes at seven."

She glanced at the watch on her wrist and hit her hand on the table. "Crud. Luke was supposed to pick me up over an hour ago. I'm really sorry," she said, gathering her books and shoving them into her bag.

"Did you need to call him?"

"No, he probably won't answer the phone. He's only managed to pick me up once this week. He's busy getting ready for Street Wars. He's probably stuck under the hood of a car right now." She zipped her book bag shut and slung it over her shoulder. "I'm really sorry for keeping you here so late. I know the library closes at seven, but I was so into my book I didn't even notice the time."

"It's OK." I had totally been there before. That was the whole reason I worked at the library, I got to be surrounded by the things I loved all day.

"I'll see ya," she waved and headed out the door.

I quickly flipped off all the lights, making sure everything was ready for tomorrow and walked out the door. "Shit," I muttered as I got pelted with rain as I locked the door. I ran to my car, looking for the girl but didn't see her. Was she really going to walk home in the rain? I glanced up and down the street and saw her two blocks up, huddled under a tree.

Whoever this Luke was who was supposed to pick her up was a complete douche monkey for making this poor girl walk. I assumed it was her father, but it was strange that she called him Luke.

I ducked into my car, tossing my purse in the back and stuck the key in the ignition. I cranked it up and reversed out of my spot. As I pulled up to the girl, all I could do was shake my head. What did she think she was doing? Standing under a tree during a thunderstorm was not a bright idea.

"Get in the car," I hollered over the wind and rain. That was one of the drawbacks of the library, there weren't many windows so I never knew what the weather was like until I went outside. "I'll give you a ride."

She shook her head no and huddled under her jacket. What was she thinking? It didn't look like the rain was going to let up anytime soon. "I'm not supposed to ride with strangers."

Well, that was all fine and dandy except for the fact me being a stranger looked a lot better than standing in the rain. "You've been coming into the library for months. I'd hardly call us strangers."

"I don't even know your name," she said, her teeth chattering.

"It's Violet. Now get in the car."

She looked up and down the street, and it finally sunk in that I was her only chance of getting home not sopping wet. As she sprinted across the street, I reached across the center console and pushed open the passenger door.

"Oh my God, it's cold out there," she shivered as she slid in and closed the door.

"Well, it's only April. Plus, being soaking wet doesn't help."

She tossed her bag on the floor and rubbed her arms, trying to warm up. I switched the heat on full blast and pointed all the vents at her. She was dripping all over, and I knew the next person who sat there was going to get a wet ass. "Which way?"

"I live over on Thompson, on top of SRK Motors," she chattered.

I shifted the car into drive and headed down the street. "How come your dad didn't come and pick you up?" I asked, turning down Willow Street.

"Probably because he's dead."

Oh, crap. Whoopsie. "I'm sorry," I mumbled, feeling like an idiot. She seemed too young to have lost her dad.

"You can rule my mom out, too. They're both dead." She pulled a dry sweatshirt out of her bag and wrapped it around her hair, wringing it out.

OK. Well, things seemed to have taken a turn for the worse. "So, um, who's Luke? Your uncle?"

"No, he's my oldest brother. I've got three of them. They all work at the garage together that Luke owns, he's in charge."

"So, your brothers take care of you?"

"Ha, more like I take care of them. If it weren't for me, they'd spend all their time under the hood of a car."

"What's your name?" Here I was giving this girl a ride home, and I had no idea what her name was.

"Frankie."

"I'm Violet, by the way, if you didn't hear me before," I glanced at her, smiling.

"Neat name. Never heard it before." That would be because my mother was an old soul who thought to name me Violet would be retro. It wasn't. It was a color.

"Eh, it's OK."

I pulled up in front of the body shop and shut the car off. It was raining even harder now, the rain pelting against my windows. "I'll come in with you to make sure someone is home."

"I'm fourteen years old. I can be left alone.'

"Whatever. Let's go." She was right, but I didn't care. I was pretty pissed off that her brother had left her all alone to walk home in the rain.

We dashed to the door, my coat pulled over my head, and I stumbled into the door Frankie held open. "Oh my God, it's really coming down," I mumbled, shaking my coat off. My hair was matted to my forehead, and I'm sure I looked like a drowned rat.

"I think Luke is in the shop, I'll go get him." Frankie slipped through another door that I assumed lead to the shop, and I looked around.

Apparently, I was in the office of the body shop. There was a cluttered counter in front of me and stacks of wheels and tires all around. Four chairs are set off to the side, which I assume is the waiting area, and a vending machine on the far wall.

The phone rang a shrilling ring, making me jump. I looked around, trying to figure out what to do when the door to the shop was thrown open, and a bald, scowling man came walking through. He didn't even glance at me, just picked up the phone and started barking into it.

"Skid Row Kings," he grunted.

I couldn't hear what was being said on the other end, but I could tell Baldy was not happy. I looked down at my hands, noticing my cute plaid skirt I had put on that morning was now drenched and clinging to my legs. Thankfully I had worn flats today, or I probably would have fallen on my ass in the rain.

"What can I help you with?"

My head shot up, baldy staring at me. "Um, I brought Frankie home."

He looked me up and down, his eyes scanning me over. "Aren't you a little too old to be hanging out with a fourteen-year-old? You're what, sixteen, seventeen?"

"Try twenty-seven." This guy was a piece of work. He was looking me over like I was on display and he thought I was a teenager.

His eyes snapped to mine, and his jaw dropped. Yeah, jackass, I'm older than you are probably. "What the hell are you doing with Frankie?"

"She works at the library. You know, the place you promised to pick me up from today?" Frankie said, walking back into the shop. She had managed to find a towel and was drying herself off. I would kill for a towel right now.

"Fuck," Baldy twisted around and looked at the clock behind him. "Sorry, Frankie. Mitch and I were tearing apart the tranny on the Charger."

She waved her hand at him and tossed the towel to me. Oh, thank you sweet baby Jesus. I wiped the water that was dripping down my face and squeezed all the water out of my hair into it.

"How the hell did you get so wet if she gave you a ride home?"

"Because I started walking home, Luke, until Violet was kind enough to stop and give me a lift."

He watched me dry my hair, confusion on his face. "Violet?" he muttered.

"That's me," I said, sticking my hand out for him to shake. "I didn't want Frankie to get sick walking home. Plus, it's getting dark and someone her age shouldn't be out then."

"She's fourteen years old," he sneered. "I was out on the streets when I was twelve."

"Oh, well. If that's how you want to raise her." Luke was a gearhead that was also an ass. I didn't have time for this. My bath was definitely calling my name now that I was soaking wet. I tossed the towel back to Frankie and pulled my jacket over my head again. "You're welcome for bringing your sister home."

"I didn't ask you to."

"I know," I turned to Frankie and smiled. "I'll see ya tomorrow." She nodded her head at me, smiling, and I turned to walk out the door. I twisted the handle, and the door blew into me, rain pouring in. I glance back at Luke one time, a scowl on his face, and figured the pouring rain was better company than he was.

I pulled the door shut behind me and sprinted to my car, dodging puddles.

Once I was safely in my car, I looked up at the two-story building and sighed. I wish I could say this was a hole in the wall garage, but it was far from that. The building itself was a dark blue aluminum siding with huge neon letters that boasted, Skid Row Kings Garage, also known as SRK Garage. There were five bay doors that I'm assuming is where they pulled the cars into and over the office part is where I believe they lived. It was monstrous. Everyone in town took their cars here, especially the street racing crowd.

I had never been here before, mainly because I have never really needed repairs done on my car. I always went to the big chain stores to get my oil changed and thankfully hadn't needed any major repairs.

I started my car, thankful to be headed home. I turned around, the big looming building in my review as I headed down the street.

Hopefully, that was the last time I would ever step foot in Skid Row Kings garage and never see Luke again. He seemed like a total ass.

= = = = = = = = = = = = =

Get a taste of the #NinjaHotties!

Dropkick My Heart

Powerhouse M.A.

Book 1

Kellan

"Left, Ryan." I shook my head and watched Ryan punch to the right. "Your other left, Ryan." In my fifteen years of teaching martial arts, I discovered left and right was a concept that was hard learned by anyone under the age of ten, especially when they were just excited to be punching and kicking the shit out of stuff.

"Okay! Lock it up." I stood in front of my class of twenty-five under belts and watched them all fall to the floor, eagerly looking up at me. I waited for all eyes to fall on me. "Good job today, guys. We need to work a bit longer on delta, but for only working on it one day, you guys are killing it." Clinton raised his hand eagerly, and I tipped my chin at him. "Go ahead, Clinton."

"Mr. Wright, when are we going to get to put all of the combos together?" he asked meekly.

"As soon as we learn them all," I assured him. Clinton asked the same question every class. The kid was the most eager to learn, but he had the attention span of a squirrel. I surveyed the class, then looked over the crowd of parents waiting to pick up their kids. "Now, remember that belt graduation is in three weeks, and you need to have your homework turned in before. Otherwise, you don't graduate." Everyone groaned at the word *homework*, and I couldn't help but smirk. They didn't have any clue how much homework I had done to reach sixth-degree black belt. "Everyone up," I said, motioning up with my hands. "And bow," I ordered, placing my hands at my sides and bowing.

All the kids started running up to me, giving me high fives and then scurrying off to their parents.

"Is Mr. Roman going to be here next time?" Carrie asked me as she high-fived me.

"He should be. He had a couple of things to do today and couldn't make it to class." Like sleeping until noon and screwing me over completely. Thankfully, it was the last class of the day, and I could hopefully find some time to sit down for five minutes.

Finally, the last parents left with their kids, and I locked the door behind them. I loved classes on Saturday, but they were exhausting when I was the only instructor.

The phone rang on the desk, and I knew it was Roman with some lame-ass excuse for why he didn't make it in today. Roman and I were business partners with Dante and Tate, but most of the time, it was all on me to make the school a success.

Roman's name flashed on the caller ID, and I picked up the phone. "So, what's your excuse this time?"

"Ugh, I'm fucking sick, man."

I shook my head and sat down behind the front counter. "That's called a hangover, Roman. Drink some fucking coffee, and get out of bed."

"Nah, man. This is worse than a hangover. I think I got food poisoning from the burger I ate last night at Tig's." Roman moaned into the phone, and I sighed.

Food poisoning from Tig's was a definite possibility. "I guess you should stop eating nasty shit while you're getting shit-faced every night."

"It's not every night," Roman grumbled.

"Sure, keep fucking telling yourself that."

Roman sighed. "Look, I was just calling to tell you sorry about not coming in today. If you wanna take off next Saturday, you can. I'll take care of the monsters all by myself."

"Nah, don't worry about." I made the mistake once of trying to take off a Saturday. Roman had called me halfway through the day, and I could barely hear him over yelling parents and screaming kids. I ended up coming in and spending most of the day putting out fires he had started between yelling at the kids and telling the parents to shut it while he was teaching. "Just get better, and I'll see you Monday night."

"What time do classes start?"

I closed my eyes and counted to ten. "Four. Same as every Monday," I reminded him.

"Got it. I'll be there."

I hung up the phone and sighed. Roman was one of the most talented guys I knew when it came to karate, but his adulting skills were severely lacking. At the age of twenty-eight, he should have his shit figured out.

When Roman, Tate, Dante, and I opened Powerhouse, we expected to help kids the way we were taught when we were young and just starting karate. Roman, Tate, and I began karate at the same time and worked our way through the belts together. Dante was a red belt when we were white belts, but he took us under his wing, and we all became close friends.

While Dante was almost ten years older than most of us, I was the highest black belt. Dante was a second-degree black belt, while Roman and Tate were fourth-degree. I was going for my sixth degree this year.

We all came together to start the school, because we all had our own specialties that, when put together, created a karate studio unlike any around. Dante was an international sparring champion six times over, while Roman and Tate were geniuses when it came to kamas and bo staff. I rounded us out with my expertise in forms and people skills the three others lacked at times.

The school had only been open for six months, but Dante and Tate already thought we needed to open another location. Not only had Roman bailed on me today, but so had Tate and Dante to go look at a space two towns over for a new studio.

I was in the minority when I said we should just focus on the Falls City school. Dante and Tate had decided between themselves that if we were doing so well here, another studio would be a goldmine. I didn't think they were wrong, I just wanted them to slow down, and wait for all of us to agree.

I threw my phone on top of a pile of new student paperwork and propped my arms on my head. I pushed off on the floor and spun around in the chair. Most days, it was hard to believe this was my life, and today was another one of those days. Dante, Tate, and Roman were my closest friends, but sometimes it felt like everything rested on my shoulders, while they were off somewhere enjoying life, and spending all the money we were making.

The days we didn't have classes, I was giving private lessons, or working on lesson plans for each class. Most of the time, the Kinder-kicker class was like herding a pack of cats that were all hyped up on catnip, and the Little Ninja class wasn't much better. Although, I still tried to teach them forms and basic karate to help them get to white belt. Once the kids hit white belt, things became more serious, and I buckled down on the curriculum.

The highest belt level we had right now was an orange belt, but in the stack of paper on the desk, there were three kids wanting to transfer over to Powerhouse. One of them was a purple belt, and the other two were red belts. I was rather shocked the two red belts wanted to transfer schools when they were close to being black belts, but I knew it was because in the short time we had been open, we already had a reputation of being the best.

If you were even a little bit into karate, you would have at least heard of one of us. We were the best, and we had the trophies and medals to prove it. That reputation was bringing in students left and right, but I couldn't keep doing this on my own anymore.

But, I wasn't going to stress about that right now, because a knock on the front door made me jump, and I turned to see my next private lesson through the glass.

My five-minute break was up, and it was back to the grind.

Someone had to make Powerhouse a success, and that someone was going to be me.

****